sewing shut
my eyes

fictions: lance olsen
computer visuals: andi olsen

FC2
A Black Ice Book
Normal/Tallahassee

Published by FC2 with support provided by Florida State University, the Unit for Contemporary Literature of the Department of English at Illinois State University, the Program for Writers of the Department of English at the University of Illinois at Chicago, and the Illinois Arts Council

Address all inquiries to: Fiction Collective Two, Florida State University, c/o English Department, Tallahassee, FL 32306-1580

ISBN: Paper, 1-57366-083-3

Library of Congress Cataloging-in-Publication Data
Olsen, Lance, 1956-
  Sewing shut my eyes / language, Lance Olsen ; computer visuals, Andi Olsen.
    p.cm.
  ISBN 1-57366-083-3 (paper)
  I. Olsen, Andi. II. Title.

PS3565.L777 S49 2000
813'.54--dc21

                              00-022338

Cover Image: Andi Olsen
Cover Design: Polly Kanevsky
Book Design: Stacey Gottlieb and Tara Reeser

Produced and printed in the United States of America
Printed on recycled paper with soy ink

Illinois ARTS Council
AN AGENCY OF THE STATE OF ILLINOIS

This program is partially sponsored by a grant from the Illinois Arts Council

ALSO BY LANCE OLSEN

NOVELS

Live from Earth
Tonguing the Zeitgeist
Burnt
Time Famine

SHORT STORIES

My Dates with Franz
Scherzi, I Believe

POETRY

Natural Selections
(With Jeff Worley)

NONFICTION

Ellipse of Uncertainty
Circus of the Mind in Motion
William Gibson
Lolita: A Janus Text
Surfing Tomorrow (Editor)
In Memoriam to Postmodernism: Essays on the Avant-Pop (Co-Editor)

TEXTBOOK

Rebel Yell: A Short Guide to Fiction Writing

ACKNOWLEDGMENTS

Industrial-strength thanks go to Jeffrey DeShell, Larry McCaffery, and Ron Sukenick for editorial feedback and support along this narratological autobahn, and to Curt White, Ralph Berry, and FC2/Black Ice Books for keeping the alternative infrastructure up and running through the heart of the Daydream Nation.

The following stories appeared previously—in slightly different form—in *Anyone Is Possible: New American Short Fiction* (Red Hen), *Caprice*, *Crimes of the Beats* (Autonomedia), *Dick for a Day* (Villard), *Fiction International*, *Fryburger*, *Fugue*, *Gargoyle*, *House Organ*, *Nobodaddies*, *Postfeminist Playground*, *Spitting Image*, *Weber Studies*, *Wisconsin Review*, and *Wordwrights*.

For Andi, collaborator 24/7...

It is in this way, under the pretext of saving the original, that the caves of Lascaux have been forbidden to visitors and an exact replica constructed 500 meters away, so that everyone can see them (you glance through a peephole at the real grotto and then visit the reconstituted whole). It is possible that the very memory of the original caves will fade in the mind of future generations, but from now on there is no longer any difference: the duplication is sufficient to render both artificial.

—Jean Baudrillard, "The Precession of Simulacra"

CONTENTS

TELEGENESICIDE

(for raymond federman)

People say Time on my hands...
but I don't have any hands. I'll
take THE PAST for a thousand.
I'll take MEMORY.
I'm a hall of fame.
I'm a classic rock station.

V I D E O R A P E

S I M U L S T

Every morning I wake up
and thank god for my unique
ability to accessorize, locate just
the right options for just the right look.

Think of all the hair colors in the world.
Think of all the brands of fingernail polish.

Fr. peine, paine, poine, pæne; peine, from L.
rly, pain, torment.]

entally, or physically, especially distress, suffering

d to pleasure.

pain, n. [ME. pa
pæna, expiation
1. originally
2.

SIGNAL-TO-NOISE
RATIO

"I am television," she said.
"Come into my body."

I change, you change, they change. Time release. Time capsule, time keeper, time...

CEREBRAL CORE TEXT

NERVOUS SYSTEM

"Oh my god!" she thought.

"Nanobots from Metaluna are singing in my tongue.

This can't be happening!

This can't be happening!"

She tried to scream but couldn't.

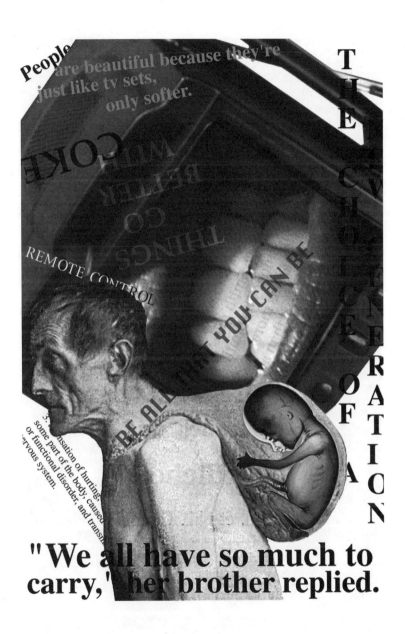

People are beautiful because they're just like tv sets, only softer.

COKE

THINGS GO BETTER WITH

REMOTE CONTROL

BE ALL THAT YOU CAN BE

THE CHOICE OF A NEW GENERATION

3. a sensation of hurting; some part of the body, caused or functional disorder; and transn... nervous system.

"We all have so much to carry," her brother replied.

She realized when she was six she was pregnant. The brother she had always wanted was growing ectopically on the wall of her intestines, product of an alien abduction. He matured slowly, several hundred thousand cells a year, among her waste. On her thirteenth birthday he became a miniature television set and began broadcasting to her through the voice-chip implanted in her tongue. "Kill dad," he said. "Show me you care." "The second-order simulacrum simplifies the problem by the absorption of appearances, or by the liquidation of the real," she replied. That night she drugged her father using chemicals found in the saliva of rare red South American tree frogs she slathered on his Big Mac. He realized what she had done, but it was too late. He collapsed at the table. It wasn't enough to kill him, though, so she rummaged through the kitchen and located a steak knife, which she inserted, once, one fourth-inch deep, into his right biceps, then ran from the house, hitchhiked into the country, and stood in the middle of a cornfield, waiting for the silver products of her imagination to beam her to a higher level of understanding. Instead she was attacked by a covey of wild cats (the wandering souls of electrocuted, hanged, and lethally injected serial killers) crazed by the scent of frog saliva, beef, and special sauce on her fingertips. She died a blind hiss-filled death. "You really love me," her brother whispered as she perished. "You love me, you love me, you love me . . ."

Television and the Triumph of Culture

–Arthur Kroker & David Cook.

Television functions

Implanting a simulated,

electronically monitored

and technocratically

controlled

identity

in the

flesh."

They are the next world.

Everything's prime time.

Everything's

Every-

thing's

within

budget.

"The schizo . . .
can no longer produce
the limits of his own being,
can no longer play nor stage himself,
can no longer produce himself as
He is now only a pure screen,
a switching center for all
the networks of influence."

–Jean Baudrillard,
"The Ecstasy of Communication"

. [pl.] the labor of childbirth.
She bowed herself and travailed; for her pains came upon her. —Sam. iv. 19.

"Let my baby live!"
she cried.

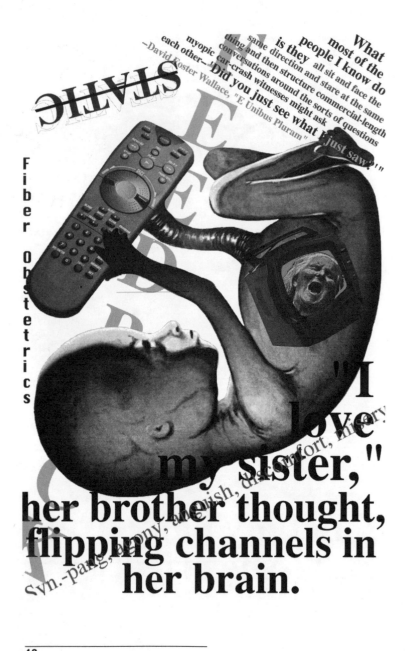

NASA, WE HAVE A PROBLEM HERE

Freak quency

INCIDENCE OF CANCER IN MEN:
skin......................23%
.al......................3%
.........................18%
co..r & 11%
other d..................10%
pros.....................10%
u.i......................7%

.CER IN WOMEN
.........................13
.........................2.
.........................3.
.........................23.
& rect..................13.
other diges.............8.
uter....................15
u.......................3.

"My mind is pain," she thought to herself, lying on her side among the stalks. "My mind is light. My mind is a cathode-ray tube. It's so beautiful I could die."

SEWING SHUT MY EYES

How Itty "The Human" Snibb Was More or Less Born Again

Itty "The Human" Snibb encountered the face of god, or at least the wed all-star notions of sublimity and the transcendental signified, at somewhere around thirty-three thousand feet above and about six miles due west of a point roughly triangulated by the towns of Iron Lightning, Thunder Butte, and Faith, South Dakota, in a part of that fortieth state so mind-numbingly flat you could in all likelihood get out of your car on the two-lane highway there in the early afternoon, unzip your bowling ball pouch, and begin rolling that ball in an easterly direction, get back in your car, drive ahead twenty miles, stop, get out, sit by the side of the road and partake of a pastrami sandwich, a beer, even a lengthy nap, and before nightfall probably catch sight of that ebony orb revolving slowly toward you silhouetted by a stunning sunset colored mandarin orange and frog green with dust airborne by the continual and sometimes pushy Great Plains breeze.

But he didn't mean to.

It was an accident, the last thing, in fact, on Itty's mind, as most people who encounter the face of god will tell you is the case, if they're being honest with themselves.

Itty "The Human" Snibb was about as undevout a guy as you can imagine, which is why among other things people called Itty "The Human" Snibb Itty *"The Human"* Snibb. They were being ironic. The truth was there appeared to be very little human about him. His head, for instance, vaguely reminded most people of a fleshy anvil turned sideways with a curl of black hair where the forehead should've been and a pair of pink sores where most people would have drawn the eyes. His fingers and toes looked more like tiny callousy hammerhead sharks than conventional fingers and toes. And his stubby thirty-three-year-old body sported just a hint of a hunchback as it struggled to stretch just a smidgen over three feet into the biosphere, miscalculating genes having done a major number on the algebra of his bones and muscles and having led Itty both to his lack of devotion and to his potent if grantedly paranoid belief that *he* was really the normal one around here and that the rest of the world was inhabited by a race of grotesque giants whose job it was to persecute him—if, that is, he didn't persecute *them* first, which, actually, he did, the only way he knew how: by going to business school, where he studied with the ferocity of a Great White bearing down on the Platonic ghost of Jacques Cousteau, and thus graduated, if not at the top of his class, then certainly high enough in the rankings to do some real damage to the U.S. economy by dressing in snappy if understandably ill-fitting suits and beginning his own chain of convenience stores called IttyBigMan's, or IBM's for short, which he built on the most desolate patches of highways he could find in places like Nebraska, Idaho, and South Dakota, patches where motorists got (with even the slightest innuendo) easily anxious about such things as starving to death and/or running out of gas and being visited by a nice-guyish serial killer stopping to lend a hand, and by sticking up a thicket of gently but steadily intimidating signs (concocted by a crack team of psychologists in Itty's employment), and by charging the unwary and mildly desperate patrons stellar prices for items nobody would buy except in limit-situations, such as those dried brown sticks of leather masquerading as meat byproducts or those dumb red plastic mugs printed with state mottoes ("Equality Before the Law," "Esto Perpetua," "Under God the People Rule") that you fill with ice water and then spill the first time you need to change lanes abruptly because of that Winnebago veering into your path like some tin-and-tire sperm whale into the path of an oncoming speedboat.

Which is what brought Itty to somewhere around thirty-three thousand feet above a point roughly triangulated by the towns of Iron Lightning, Thunder Butte, and Faith: he was in the process of flying from his home base on a barren bump in the cornfields of mid-Illinois to a franchise-owners convention in a low-slung motel somewhere in the central wastelands of Washington State for the purpose of receiving a silver plaque in recognition of his ground-breaking concept of Anxiety Purchasing, and he'd been awake all night with his stable of PR men drafting his acceptance speech, which began "I guess what I've got to say is that I don't really feel I deserve this award, but, then, I am almost one-hundred-and-ten inches tall and have a hunchback and I don't really feel I deserve these things either," and which went on to insinuate in the most charming terms possible the presence of a vast conspiracy of lanky people whose mission was to undermine the confidence and financial success of short people throughout the world by doing stuff like making sinks just high enough so the faucets were out of reach and manufacturing chairs so far off the ground that short people like Itty never looked credible at board meetings. The outcome of his sleeplessness was not only a golden-tongued oration bound to garner yet more media attention for his fast-growing string of IBM's, with the needless-to-say concomitant rise in quarterly earnings, but also a champion case of the flu, mean as that monster in *Alien* who dribbled, snarled, and made a mess of the spaceship, not to mention Sigourney Weaver's buddies, which gestated in Itty's unwitting bowels as he showered and shaved at dawn, multiplied and glided in viral flotillas through his bloodstream as his very tall very handsome chauffeur drove him to the airport, sun flaming the horizon white and blue like the first frozen instant of a nuclear explosion, and birthed resoundingly as the DC-10 lifted its nose wheel from the tarmac at O'Hare, rattling for altitude and sending a pitbull of nausea yipping through Itty's consciousness a nanosecond before he felt his sphincter involuntarily relax just as he flipped to the business section of *World News* in first class and wondered whether or not he should order that glass of champagne to accompany his poached-egg-and-sausage breakfast which would be arriving any minute.

The answer, proffered by his gut that had instantaneously spiraled into a Mobius strip, then into an intricate origami of pain, and finally into a complex map of the LA freeway system gushing with frantic traffic all trying to reach the same intersection in nine seconds or less, was no. Everything in his body simultaneously turned liquid: hot, bubbling, expanding liquid; and this liquid then turned into gas, the gas into steam, and the steam into super-heated vapors pent in a vessel three thousand times too small to contain them. The sores that were Itty's eyes brimmed with tears, the anvil that was his head with multitudinous special-effects pyrotechnics, and the spirit of anguish (dressed as a frothing Hell's Angel complete with skull-and-crossboned black leather jacket and black-and-silver steel-tipped boots) raged into his viscera wielding a blowtorch in one hand and a chainsaw in the other. Itty dropped his magazine and tilted up his chin as though the thought of prayer had suddenly swept through his being (although it hadn't, yet) and, opening and closing his mouth like a blowfish in an aquarium, he reached down with trembling fingers and delicately unfastened his seat belt, cautious with the latch as the guy on the bomb squad who's been disarming those gizmos for thirty-three years and now knows

the only thing that stands between him and a safe retire-
ment to a chaise lounge by a blue pool in the courtyard of a
Floridian condo at four o'clock on a sunny February afternoon is this one small fuse connected to this one inordi-
nately large bundle of TNT.

And then the real discomfort began. It felt like someone had decided to perform hara-kiri on Itty from the inside out with a fistful of dull razor blades, each dipped in
high-grade carbolic acid, and that this someone couldn't
make up his mind where to begin cutting first, so he tried
everywhere at once, which would have been just fine, except he was drunk and in a bad mood and had brought
along for the ride six hundred and sixty-six of his closest,
most ornery confreres, all of them drunker and in worse
moods than himself. It felt, in certain almost unspeakable
ways, like the DC-10 on which Itty currently traveled was
no longer surrounding him, containing him in its dry cabin
always a little too cool or a little too warm and scented with
sour jet fuel, rubbery seat cushions said to double as life
vests (though, as Itty often noted to himself as he first willed
the plane into the air and then willed it to stay there, didn't
exactly exude a sense of confidence in those sitting on them),
and foiled food that smelled like no other food on earth,
foiled or unfoiled, smelled, supporting him five miles over
what now must have been Cedar Rapids, Iowa, but instead
that the plane had somehow imploded into itself and then
into his belly, where it had accelerated, unleashing the gar-
gantuan flame throwers of its multiple engines on the sensitive membranes of Itty's inner self, nuking his entrails,
boiling his duodenum in its own juices, cauterizing his anus
so that he almost lost sensation there, the sensation so powerful, as he inched out of his seat, slipped to the floor, and
shuffled into the aisle, unaware of virtually everything going on around him in the same way a voodoo priest walking on Jujubes of coals at a big voodoo priest ritual is unaware of virtually everything going on around him—the
pale blue carpet he tread upon, the interested faces of the

other passengers confronted by this well-dressed first-class midget with a deadly serious glare etched into each and every one of his warped features, the blond-bunned flight attendant he pushed past without so much as one of his quick practiced leers at her tight ass (which was, per usual, floating with unavoidable facticity at eye-level) in order to demonstrate to the world that he was as libidinous and slimy as the next guy, short or not—trying as he did to maintain his composure those last ten feet and seven seconds it would take him to attain the lavatory, those last three yards and six seconds it would take him before he could slam and lock that flimsy aluminum door behind him, wrench down his pants and underwear, and scramble into position before the voiding of his essence began, with or without his consent, in a humid rush beneath him. He discovered himself actually *anticipating* his arrival by several heartbeats with the pretty pathetic gesture of prematurely extending his right arm and spreading his fingers as though he were some magician willing the lavatory door to open, the pressurized cabin seeming to make the gaseous agony punishing his midgut increase to an extent where he knew that if he didn't hurry he ran the risk of blowing up on the spot in a putrid cloud of bodily fluids; and so, while not exactly breaking into a full sprint, Itty sort of hopped, skipped, and dashed the last yard, gripping the knob no bigger than a fifty-cent piece and twisting it with almost reverent intensity, the understanding now fibrillating in that place in one's soul where devotion is kept that a whoosh of freedom awaited him within a matter of instants almost too small to count.

Only it was locked. The knob was locked. The little plastic oblong slab on the lavatory door said OCCUPIED.

Itty stared dumbfounded, moving his mouth in surprise, snaking out his neck from his rigid collar as if he were going to lick the thing, and doing a fine brief jig while thirteen lifetimes catsuped by before he comprehended what he was looking at, at which point an earthquake of

horror shuddered over his countenance. He stopped danc-
ing. He retracted his neck. His pink eyes became, if possible, pinker, took on the wet, glaucous appearance of ob-
jects left in the hold of a sunken ship way too long, and he
involuntarily lifted himself onto his toes, his body strain-
ing for height, then lowered himself back onto his heels,
partially because he thought better of this first action, given
his propensity for self-esteem, partially because another
jumbo jet was taxiing down the runway of his colon. The
abrupt pangs accompanying its takeoff bent him at the
waist, transmogrifying him into a prim European psychia-
trist meeting his latest hysteric in a 1902 drawing room,
and then rotated his head so that he peered over his right
shoulder and down the aisle like Wile E. Coyote knowing,
just knowing, that that big boulder he'd catapulted at the
Road Runner a minute ago had misfired and was presently
sailing up the desert canyon toward him, seconds to im-
pact, and that there was nothing, nothing whatsoever, he
could do about it.

Except it wasn't a big boulder he saw when he peered
over his right shoulder: it was a compartment abob with
curious faces waiting to see what the funny dwarf would
do next. Which, it so transpired, was (all the self-esteem
business pretty much out the porthole by now) to scurry
back down the aisle as fast as his imperfect legs could carry
him, panic floreating in his mucoidal eyes, past all those
pale faces that made him feel a little bit like a mobile in-
flight movie screen, keenly aware that a dramatic tension
had just invaded his sphincter, announcing either (if there
was a god) the advent of a small bashful passing of breathtakingly stale wind or (if there was not) the onslaught of a
vile torrent of watery filth, through the curtain separating
first class from second, and right into the towering food
cart serving minuscule plastic rectangles, each dabbed with
artificial eggs, a large comma that might have been a strip
of bacon or a sliver of badly burned wood, and that inex-
plicable dark green leaf of lettuce everyone tacitly agrees

no one has to touch, none of which Itty's psyche recorded because Itty was busy clambering into the lap of a startled woman wearing a powder-blue leisure suit and synthetic cotton-candy hair, hoisting himself onto her seatback and vaulting into the aisle on the other side of that cart, using this newly-created momentum to propel himself (tearing loose his belt buckle and fumbling with the buttons on his pants as he moved) through the myriad shouts of disbelief to the threshold of the one empty lavatory at the rear of the airplane, whose door Itty threw open and clapped shut behind him with a high-pitched nearly animal-like groan of relief.

Itty "The Human" Snibb had planned to do many things that morning, had planned, for instance, to read the business section of that *World News* he'd just left spread behind him on his comfy leatherette seat like a shot gray-and-white bird, mutely rehearse his acceptance speech while sipping champagne, catnap both to retrieve some sleep lost the night before and ease the jetlag awaiting his arrival just beyond baggage claim at the Spokane airport, wake to a cup of sweet coffee and cream before beginning the smooth descent toward the hour-and-a-half limo drive west that would end in an amazingly level black parking lot belonging to that low-slung motel, itself the product of a franchise, somewhere on a dead scrubby patch of sizzling summer highway between Almira and Hartline; but now, spasmodically erupting as that blond-bunned flight attendant rapped diffidently at the door and inquired if there were anything she might do to ease his misery, too overrun with his body's riot to reply, able only to bring forth a few juicy gasps like some suffocating cold-victim in the throes of a world-class sinus attack while rocking side to side and back to front on the (even to him) constrictive toilet seat stuck in the constrictive phone booth that passed for a lavatory on the DC-10, cramps ramrodding his intestines like a team of narcotics agents at the portal of a crack house at two in the morning, temples pressurizing for detonation with cartilage-ripping exertions that resounded through his torso like savage miniature plate tectonics on a particularly busy day in the Pacific rim, Itty was reminded of something his mother, Millie, also a delicately hunchbacked dwarf, and also in something approaching a continual state of metaphysical PMS (due in large part to the fact that her husband, Hal, a circus clown with a propensity for the bizarre, left her after six years of fairly blissful marriage and astoundingly creative sex for a tall svelte trapeze artist twice Millie's height and only two-thirds her weight), told him from the time he was three in that crummy trailer park on the outskirts of Beaverville, Illinois, where he suddenly came to consciousness one leafy autumn afternoon in 1963, that if you want to see god laugh all you have to do is tell him what your plans are.

Simultaneously, however, somewhere deep in the intricate infrastructure of his brainstem, Itty realized with warm comfort that the worst had already passed, the most awful was already slowly gathering not before but behind him, things could only and would only improve from this blink of an eye forward, leaving him nothing save the selfless act of surrendering wholly to the wretched blood-dimmed swamp gurgling and belching beneath him, dabbing the sweat from his damp brow, and exploring with Zen-like detachment the multifarious combinations of searing woe that can be heaped upon a mortal—all of which ultimately would have been true, given another three-quarters of an hour or so, sixty minutes tops, had not a certain computer operator named Wally Klott at the NASA tracking center in Houston three years earlier fallen seriously in love with a certain co-worker named Matilda Weingarten, flinching as he began to stand one day because Mattie happened just then to stroll past his cubicle, glorious hips swaying (if you use your imagination, which Wally did) beneath her baggy navy-blue slacks, strawberry helmet of hair catching the light in a fluorescent shimmer, and to actually say "Hiya, Wally, what's up?" which sent poor Wally Klott right over the amorous edge, causing him to knock his nearly full cup of heavily NutraSweetened coffee atop his console onto its side with a brown splash, splutter, and hiss that flatlined his system instantaneously and sent an electronic coronary galloping into earth's orbit at the speed of radio waves directly into the soul of MURMA-5, a small weather satellite in geosynchronous spin above, more or less, Devil's Tower, Wyoming, that Wally had been monitoring, thereby affecting its trajectory by less than a gnat's left eyebrow's follicle, which didn't seem like all that terribly much at the time, especially since Wally flicked off his unit immediately, but which can really add up over a couple of million seconds when no one notices the mistake initially and then the strangeness of the satellite's rotation can't easily be corrected when one does notice it (the one being, in this case, Mattie herself, thirteen months after the fact, and two weeks and two days after she and Wally finally consummated their budding relationship in a chlorine-scented stall of the women's restroom at the NASA tracking center in Houston amid much klutzing around with snaps and zippers, and many apologies for brevity, environmentally induced asthma, and faulty aim), which strangeness over the course of those three years tilted MURMA-5 right into the maiden traces of earth's frictive atmosphere and hence into a wild wobble which gravity, being gravity, just ate up, tore apart, sucked right down into the stratosphere, where the MURMA-5 plain disintegrated, or virtually plain disintegrated, broadcasting red-hot fragments of itself hither and yon, one of which (no bigger than Itty's fist, still clenched in somber concentration as a scalding café-noir rivulet squirted from him) rocketed toward a recently cut bale of hay hulking like a gigantic beige Tootsie Roll in a farm field one mile west of Lebanon, South Dakota, on a course that would have completely obliterated that bale in a megalithic fulmination of unsuspecting mice, an intensely malicious tabby poised for the pounce, and a conflagration that would've ignited this field and the next two over, threatening the nearby town with extinction for the better part of an afternoon, till firefighters from three counties finally showed up with some important-looking firefighting equipment—except that on its way down it struck the first-class section of the DC-10 instead, ripping a yard-wide hole in its fuselage and creating the hugest intake-of-breath sound most of the passengers have probably ever heard.

This at the precise instant Itty, having briefly regained his equilibrium, parted his lips to answer the flight attendant who was querying him about the state of his affliction from the other side of the lavatory door. In place of the *no* he'd been preparing to utter in response to her fairly moronic question, followed by a peremptory *so fuck off,* all he could manage was the *uh* part of *uh-oh* before the door burst open and Itty promptly became a semi-human projectile. Still in a sitting position, pants bunched around his ankles like a pile of dead bats, effluents materializing behind him like some kind of indelible-ink trail he would later be able to follow home, Itty soared down the aisle toward the scrap of china-blue sky seemingly painted in the fuselage. While it would definitely be an overstatement to assert that Itty understood exactly what was happening, it is nonetheless clear that at some intuitive level of awareness, like that of a kid watching a horse stuck on a barbed-wire fence smear past the backseat window of his parents' car on an interstate at dusk, he gleaned various haunting sense impressions as he barreled through the tornado of magazines, styrofoam-cup shreds, glints of wire-rimmed glasses ripped from the faces of astonished lawyers as they reached to adjust them, shrunken pillows, baby blankets, wet gleams of recently extracted dentures, egg bits, dented cans of Diet 7-Up, bacon flecks, plastic trays, gold pens, cries of shock, oxygen masks shivering in the titanic aspiration, loose rhinestone earrings, clouds of airborne liquids, a forest of those untouched leaves of lettuce, someone's calculator, rumpled cowboy hats, one of those seat cushions said to double as a life vest (which Itty tried to grab, and failed), snowballs of paper and crumpled napkins, Christmas ornaments of tinfoil, a lone leather-thonged sandal, a dingy prosthetic arm, a flicker of Stephen King novels, pink sweaters undulating like flamingos on extended wings, a green vortex of ten- and twenty-dollar bills, belts that suddenly became snakes, umbrellas that suddenly became spears, shopping bags that suddenly became headgear, rapidly scattering decks of cards, miniature liquor bottles, laptop computers, a carmine-faced Englishman flapping from an overhead bin, and, most immediate for Itty, the tight ass (now covered only by a pair of boring white Fruit-of-the-Loom panties so thinned from use that Itty could even at this velocity and remoteness make out the rose tattoo adorning her taut tanned left cheek floating with unavoidable facticity at eye-level) of the flight attendant who wore her skirt inside-out and over her upper torso as if she'd dressed herself today with the intent of walking on her hands, and who was now whizzing nine feet in front of him as Itty tried unsuccessfully to unfreeze the leer frozen on his face till, in a sort of impetuous leap of faith, he was surrounded by pearly white and icy blue and it struck him that he was no longer *inside* the DC-10, which had begun what was euphemistically referred to by Dan Rather later that day on the *CBS Evening News* as a twenty-thousand foot "controlled dive," but *outside* it, hovering in frigid nothingness, the rumble of the jet's engines rapidly receding.

And then he was falling, plummeting through bright opalescence, dropping through crystallized vapors, his heart lurching in the prisonhouse of his chest as though deciding it was going to try to save itself, fuck Itty, it was getting the hell out of here, and his bladder figuring what was going on and joining his heart and intestines in their respective attempts at evacuation. Meanwhile Itty began climbing an invisible ladder, scrabbling for altitude, kicking against emptiness with his shiny black wing-tips (despite his bunched pants acting alternately like a cotton version of the chain binding together a convict's legs and a bantam parachute trembling in the stupendously noisy wind), his runted arms pistons, his lungs clusters of grapes huffing the thin air with the rapidity of a hummingbird's wings, and, at the instant he thought maybe, just *maybe,* he could make some real progress here through the sheer force of his imagination, he blacked out and twined into a dream in which he was driving down a narrow road in northern Scotland (where he'd never been, nor particularly wanted to be) in a rented rubiate Fiat on a cold rainy day at the very second eight sheep clattered out of oyster-white fog, dirty squat rectangular bodies, stubby black legs, rumps raised in defiance against him, and halted there, expectant, behind them a ditch, an incline, a row of evergreens, then moors sliding into ashen light; and, when in unison the black masks lowered warily to sniff the cracked asphalt, Itty slowly reached for his camera in the seat beside him though at the same instant one of the sheep raised its head and the others followed, their chests kicking forward, and Itty understood what he would later find in his photograph even though he decided to take it anyway: a still landscape through his windshield, trees, fog, horizon the hue of unclean bones, and a spare road winding nowhere.

He peered between his legs, around the ruffling carcass of his chubby white penis and quivering billows of his black trousers, and blinked. Upside down, he was squinting directly into the sun which was in the process of bullying the rest of the sky into paying attention to it. Everything was bathed in arctic blue light suffused with a scintillating golden fog. Itty's hammerhead fingers were numb, his ears (predictably much too small for his head) fragile as the flimsy layer of ice that epidermizes a pond after only one day of snow in late November and aswarm with his own panicked breathing. He had a strong hunch that the gelatinous liquid filming his eyes had frozen solid, and he was just beginning to contemplate the ramifications of this potentially compelling fact when he discovered himself instead examining a poor pale imitation of a vast canvas by Mondrian, geometric shapes plotted beneath him all the way to the horizon, bleached green rectangles, whitish squares, beige rhomboids, and it occurred to him he was in a slow tumble through the afternoon. Across some of the configurations networked turquoise and brown dendrites. Tiny tin barn roofs glittered at the edges of others. He could just make out the one-street assembly of erasers and thimbles that was (if he'd been in a position to consult a map) Iron Lightning, as well as the pinpricks of sunlight waterbugging on the rural road straight as a Prairie State county line that sliced across the landscape beneath his feet. It was difficult for him to comprehend how depressingly fast all this was coming into focus, how quickly the atmospheric shades of blue were darkening from cornflower toward ultramarine, how swiftly the planet was swooping up to shake his pygmied hand, but it was as simple as the tint of his black hair corkscrewing from his forehead how unlucky he would have been had he not at that moment happened to glance up from his ever-accelerating freefall to behold, perhaps some three hundred feet east of him, the tanned body of the flight attendant who, less than a minute ago, had been rapping on his lavatory door and asking, in a sense, if she might share his travail.

Itty didn't know that her name was Sharon Weingarten, nor that she was the sister of Matilda Weingarten, the woman who with the help of Wally Klott had set in motion this Rube Goldberg contraption of terrible luck, nor that she had grown up not nine miles north of Itty's hometown of Beaverville, Illinois, in Aroma Park, her one childhood wish having been to attain escape velocity from that dull rat's hole of a dung heap, as she mixed-metaphorically conceptualized it, nor even that this very morning she had performed various intricate perversities (that, if brought to court in the state of South Dakota, would prove punishable by jail terms of not longer than, respectively, six months, three years, and half a decade, with the

possibility of early parole in each case) with a young bisexual computer analyst with this cute way of fingering
his ear lobe when he talked who she'd picked up in a Chicago bar the night before and who was at this instant on
his lunch break in a broom closet of the Lakeshore Drive
office building where he worked boffing an even younger
computer analyst (not bisexual in the least) whom he'd been
hitting on for months, a little tackily if not just short of pretty
disgustingly harassingly, unknowingly gifting him with
various transmissible (though not, as the battery of tests
would later confirm, deadly) sexual diseases he'd con-
tracted just hours before at the O'Hare Airport Hilton from
none other than Sharon Weingarten herself, who was, even
as she fell, oblivious of them, thanks last week to that jerk
of a first officer with the pouty lower lip who flew the
O'Hare-Dulles route and made you feel more base than a
python's belly if you ever refused him even a cherry
LifeSaver. No. All Itty knew was that her hair, now
unbunned, bloomed above her head in a tongue of blond
flame as she plunged, that her uniform was gone (as was
for that matter Itty's soiled shirt, thin black tie, cufflinks,
and, now that he gave it some thought, his left wing-tip
shoe), having been ripped off by the supreme vigor of her
meteoric descent, so that she currently wore nothing but
those endearingly frayed Fruit-of-the-Loom panties which
complemented what with great statistical probability was
a matching Fruit-of-the-Loom bra, though of course Itty
couldn't discern the brand name—all of which made her
look horribly unprotected, bone-crackingly cold, like someone you should put your arms around immediately and
nuzzle and warm.

Which, his heart once more netted like a rare African
butterfly and drawn down his esophagus, Itty did, or tried
to do, by effecting a sort of tenacious sidestroke in her general direction, closing the space between them by perhaps
three-quarters of a yard before a muscular gust of wind
punched him back another ninety feet and caused him to

doublecheck his relationship to the earth which was presently above his anvilic head, only to have this dawn on him: that he could already make out individual patches of purple sage amoebaing across dead spans of dirt, and shadowy movement behind windshields of swiftly enlarging pickups stirring cotton balls of dust into the atmosphere as they glided along the rural road now above him, now below, not a propitious sign by anyone's standards, while Itty briefly righted himself again and located Sharon and this time serendipitously caught her eye, or at least sincerely believed he did (the azulene vacancy separating them being expansive), for what might have been if he were exceptionally generous something like seven seconds, but which seven seconds were somehow plenty long enough, given his situation, given the way just about everything had been heretofore going, because in that millennium he realized something that changed his life.

He realized that Sharon's face wasn't shockingly terrified by the negative theology whirling around it, wasn't tugged into one of those classical tragic masks by the unutterable surreality of this particular interval in her life, as Itty might have guessed, no, but was fabulously calm, fabulously composed, her gaze steady, her eyes (quite possibly parrot green, and, if they weren't in fact parrot green, should have been) unsurprised by where she happened to find herself right now and why, as if like a dolphin skimming the shockwaves of a ship's bow she had already adapted her body and mind to this new environment and made some kind of important decision about her place in its ecosystem, which realization had an instantly soothing effect on Itty, who kicked into his sidestroke again and swam toward her and (suddenly) the idea of love, only again to be clipped by a scud of wind. He paused, caught his breath (as best he could), and thrust out once more, imagining himself a salmon nosing upstream, but it didn't do much good, the wind being not unlike a logging truck hustling a Pinto off a highway, and yet, somehow, he kept his gaze connected to hers for five seconds, six, maybe even seven, and, in the end, just as the notion invaded Itty's brain that maybe he was misreading this picture, that maybe she wasn't so much *unsurprised* as *ultimately* surprised, maybe not so much *serene* as, well, *stunned,* Sharon wowed him for the last time. Although it remained hard to tell for sure from this hefty distance, Itty was ninety-nine-and-nine-tenths percent convinced that she smiled at him, *smiled,* that her lips parted, that her teeth caught the sun in a genuinely humane salute, just a millisecond before she stretched her arms over her head as though about to yawn, palm greeting palm, bent at the waist, touched her toes, and gracefully somersaulted into a streamlined swan-dive toward that point of land roughly triangulated by the towns of Iron Lightning, Thunder Butte, and Faith, South Dakota, leaving an astonished if transiently content Itty rotating like a splayed starfish increasingly far above her.

And then it was over. Or almost over. The rest played like a quick rill of notes, sense impressions flitting past rapidly as a video cassette locked on fastforward. The sky darkened. The air warmed. The planet lunged. Sharon disappeared and Itty gained sight of a sparsely populated rectangular parking lot, a gray shoeboxish building in its center, a bright silver set of gas pumps on a nearby cement island, a large sign (red letters on white) warning no more gas nor food for eighty miles, and, in his last dizzying reeling wink, this also: two tall monitor lizards in ski masks black as bowling balls sprinting from the entrance followed a split second later by a squat lump of bread dough wielding a broomstick, shotgun, or baseball bat (it was hard to tell which at this speed) whom Itty, despite his most ardent last gestures to the contrary, including a quickly mouthed prayer to the effect that if he survived this seemingly final tribulation he swore, *swore,* he would become the human his middle name had always implied, targeted with unintentional ease and actually pile-drove two feet through the sidewalk just out front of the glass doors pastiched with

polychromatic ads for mouthwatering beef jerkies, delicious
corndogs, spicy buffalo wings, day-glo sun-visors, orangish
marshmallow peanuts, cheap wristwatches, rattlesnake
paperweights, inflatable neck pillows, cartoon-character
key-chains that lauded the sexual prowess of their owners,
and sweatshirts saying things like MY PARENTS VISITED
THE BLACK MOUNTAINS AND ALL I GOT WAS THIS
STUPID SWEATSHIRT that led into the Iron Lightning-
Faith IttyBigMan's, or IBM's, for short.

PENTAPOD FREAK NEST

... much as if an animal should enwrap itself in a highly exaggerated fold of its own skin ...

CHEMICAL COMPOSITION
OF A NEWBORN INFANT

Component:	Percentage:
Water	66.0
Proteins	16.0
Fats	12.5
Carbohydrates	0.5
Minerals:	5.0

Minerals are the largest mineral constituents of the body, calcium and phosphorus, the components of bone.

PRIMITIVE STREAK

"I was very lonely," she said, "so I dreamed myself a brother."

I remember the old Branden-
burgh Museum in Philadel-
phia where for the price of
one dime—ten cents—you
could see Jo Jo, the Dog-
faced Boy; Plutano and Wai-
no, the Original Wild Men
of Borneo; Laloo from India
with his twin growing out
of his body; Arthur Loose,
the Rubber-Skinned Man who
pulled out his cheeks eight
inches and let them snap
back into place; and the
famous Mrs. Tom Thumb. The
popularity of the freaks
carried the show, but various vaudeville performers,
not yet good enough for the
Palace or Roxy's in New
York, were used as fillers.
Among the people who got
their start there were Al
Jolson, Harry Houdini,
Buster Keaton and Van
Alsyne. . . . Though these
men did well later on, it
was always the freaks whom
people came to see.
       —Daniel P. Mannix, Freaks:
       We Who Are Not As Others

"Heart of my heart," she said. "Mind of my mind."

the strange sex lives of Siamese twins

"The *body of the penis* is the part between the root and the extremity. In the flaccid condition of the organ it is cylindrical, but when erect has a ...gular prismatic form with rounded ...the broadest side being turned ...nd called the *dorsum*. The ...vered by integument, and ...ts interior a large portion ...thra. The integument ...enis is remarkable for ...ts dark color, its ...nection with deeper ...and its containing
—Gray's Anatomy

the
human torso
who could
sew,
crochet,
and type

the dwarf clown's wife whose feet grew directly from her body

the tragedy of Betty Lou Williams and her parasitic twin

the notorious love affairs of midgets

"We had always wanted to be freaks of nature, and now we'd got our wish."

40

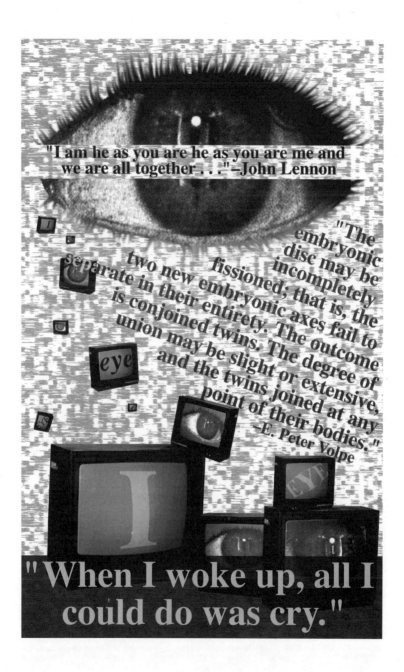

"I am he as you are he as you are me and we are all together . . ."–John Lennon

"The embryonic disc may be incompletely fissioned; that is, the two new embryonic axes fail to separate in their entirety. The outcome is conjoined twins. The degree of union may be slight or extensive, and the twins joined at any point of their bodies."
–E. Peter Volpe

"When I woke up, all I could do was cry."

Digital Matrix: Barbie: Lust

SEATTLE:BARBIE:OMEGA

Alexis, split ends of her dyed candy-apple-red hair tickling her elbows, bright white undershirt flashing beneath her unbuttoned baggy burgundy flannel shirt, sack of groceries balancing precariously in each thin arm, tripped over herself (those glossy black combat boots of hers two sizes too large and yet the smallest the store she visited carried when she decided she desperately, desperately needed a pair) as she entered the door of her multi-latched second-floor apartment in the artsily grubby if fringily dynamic Capitol Hill section of Seattle ten minutes late (the express line at the corner market being these days slow as a fat mucousy slug on a cold morning floor), took one look at Flynn slumping in front of the tv in his shredded underwear and yellowish socks, alternately channel surfing and working to free something potentially interesting he'd just discovered atop his shaved pate, and saw when he turned to welcome her with a reflexive plaque-filled smile in mid-pick, not the guy she had happily moved in with two years ago in a typhoon of lust after meeting two months earlier at this finger-gnawingly wild party (which, if the truth be known, she only dimly remembered these days) at a gallery-loft on gray-and-brick Tenth Street where she was just then showing the first triptychs from her Barbie series (*Barbie Meets Charlie Manson on Speed, Barbie Meets Alien Shortly After the Death of Her Really Special Babies at the Hands of Sigourney Weaver, Barbie Meets Kurt Cobain in Drag When He's In a Very Bad If Not Heroin-Induced Mood*) and where Flynn, once adorable Flynn, was trying to pocket this dead bird he'd recently discovered in a corner behind an assemblage involving tiny cages, glistening dentures, and various other minuscule thingumabobs, a sparrow or something, Flynn not especially good at naming anything that didn't with some regularity appear in cities and have a metallic component or hard drive, thinking maybe he'd caused it somehow to fall from said assemblage, one of the most genuinely vulnerable and bewildered grins on that five-o'clock-shadowed deliverer-of-cigarettes-to-various-vending-machines-around-town face of his you are ever likely to see, but rather someone who'd gone rosy and pudgy around the middle, thin and shiny along the widening widow's peaks, and lazy after work to an almost vegetative degree in that fuschia futon in front of that fucking tv beneath that rad poster of Blackwater Scabies, the technoguerre band he played in with decreasing frequency, if still lip-service passion, originally intent on creating the-first-on-their-block mixed media extravaganza fusing computer-enhanced industrial noise (you should have seen Flynn at his Macintosh keyboard in those early days, fingers fast and graceful as Glenn Gould unfurling his rendition of *Goldberg Variations*), performance art (many ball bearings and clouds of what might pass for diesel fuel becoming airborne in the general direction of the generally stoned audience), and recitations of free verse so disgusting and caustically arch ("let me chew your tumor, babe,/ and watch it bleed/ all over my nice new Van Heusen shirt ...") that it would redefine the very concepts of chic cynicism and flip irony, now content instead to blip from one tapeworm of jazzy images to the next until he fell into a chin-spittling sleep around ten, when the local anchor people opened their mouths in unison—and so Alexis just set down those groceries in the cramped kitchen smelling vaguely of onions no matter what air freshener she employed and returned to the cramped living room where she suggested maybe a little too strongly ("Get the fuck out of my head, Flynn") that they spend some time apart, beginning in another twenty minutes or so, and (here was the thing she'd always relive from that moment like a very bad case of flashback blues) Flynn, without so much as a snort of surprise, clicked off the remote control, stood, stuck his right hand down his underpants, itched his incrementally more cellulited butt, and said: "So did you like get the munchies or what?"

LOVE IS A BULLET

The thing that just pissed the everlasting daylights out of her was that, no matter how much she pleaded with her memory of him, no matter how much she begged that warty green neckless ogre drooling in the dark slimy corner of her psyche, double-jointed thumb exploring its left nostril, to leave, she just couldn't get even an eyebrow-flick of its attention. God knows she tried. She really *did* try. Except, of course, for those weak-spirited spans so late at night that the sky beyond her curtainless windows began ashening toward dawn, and Alexis's bladder sloshed, saturated and awash in an ocean of urine, and she grumpily struggled from that fuschia futon and shuffled into the bathroom, and then upon her return to bed couldn't no matter what she did skate back into the serene carpeted corridors of sleep because nostalgia bustled in with its big noisy bag of party favors and hunkered at the foot of her mattress in this huge, ugly, hunch-backed, slobbering, carbuncular sort of way. She had to accept the progressively obvious fact that love was a bullet fired pointblank by some cosmic Mark

David Chapman into her solar plexus, that it just lodged there, upsetting her biorhythms something awful, and that, even though its main charge might have been spent during that first instant, hot fragments of its remains shifted uneasily among her soggy organs as she bent to untie her combat boots every evening, extended her left hand to mix two dabs of pungently colored acrylics every morning. Because, if the truth be known, she had after all just spent the last two years, the last twenty four months, the last one hundred and four weeks with a guy who knew exactly how to tickle her hard enough so she almost wet her pants yet tenderly enough so that things never turned really malicious, a guy who remembered at least one out of the two birthdays they spent together, brought her that duet of roses when she got so sick with the flu she furled up under a burial mound of quilts, blankets, and pillows, and waited to expire. Who even the most die-hard skeptic had to admit at least once upon a time possessed the cutest little buns, the sugariest little boyish smile, the raddest patchouli scent behind his earlobes and beneath his jaw. Not to mention some major, *major* genius with respect to sexual stratagems and music-making. And yet and yet and yet: Flynn *was* just a guy, okay? He had that male pouty-disarmingly-helpless manipulation business down to a kind of high art form. And his deportment had pretty much evaporated in most matters worth talking about. Save for those hand-slapping-walls sexual stratagems, which once, damn it (but *only* once), drove her back to his bed this single exceptionally existentially shitty night three weeks after their initial breakup, and ended with him asking her, Alexis's head resting upon his chest, "So does this like mean we're together again or something?" And, heck, she told herself: she had had other guys in the past, she would have other guys in the future, some worse and some better than Flynn (afraid of course with each union of what sort of infectious disease might ring her up half

a decade later to say hiya, sweet thing, we're thinking of you), and that's just how life worked itself out.
Wasn't it?

MOMENTS OF TRUTH

> **BIG ROOM, THE.** n. World found outside computer installations.
> **GREP.** vt. To rapidly scan a file looking for a particular string or pattern. By extension, to look for something by pattern.
> **HEISENBUG.** n. A bug that disappears or alters its behavior when one attempts to probe or isolate it.
> **KNOTHOLE EFFECT.** n. In which you can see more if you don't look directly.
> **MEAT.** n. The stuff that stays behind when one enters cyberspace.
> **NEOPHILIA.** n. The trait of being excited and pleased by novelty. Common trait of most hackers.
> **WAVE A DEAD CHICKEN.** vt. To perform a ritual over crashed software in the hopes of reviving it.
> **WORM.** n. A computer virus that replicates itself across a network.

ONE HUNDRED GAMES OF SOLITAIRE

And so it was time to move on. Time to put this phase of her life behind her. Time to be mature, responsible, and all that stuff. She thus did what any self-respecting person in her position would do. She bobbed her hair, shaved a swath above her left ear, and dyed the resulting skewed mop from candy-apple red to wine purple. She bought a pair of olive-plaid Keds and packed up her futon, tv, pots, pans, bedding, silverware, fake tattoos (Alexis sometimes wore a black press-on skull-and-crossbones above her small right breast, three black press-on tears spilling from the corner of her breadmold-gray left eye), and art supplies, and she moved to a tinier and cheaper multi-latched third-floor apartment three blocks away with this excellent view of dumpsters, phone lines, and warehouse rooftops bristling with antennae and translucent skylights.

Not long afterward, she raised her head and realized she was deep into a new series of triptychs based on Barbie's buddy, Ken (*Ken Sails into Hell, Ken Creates Barbiestein in His Own Image, Ken Is a Serial Killer*), working sometimes till three in the morning, no longer having to worry much about disturbing a mate's dreams or television viewing habits, breakfasting at four a.m. and sleeping till two the next afternoon, keen on the fresh direction her art was carrying her, and, not long after *that*, she surprised herself by enrolling (just for the hell of it, really) in this computer-design course she'd been thinking about taking for years and years at the nearby university, penetratingly aware of how breathtakingly close to the ebony edge of twenty-three she currently teetered, how intricate life had suddenly become, how fast she sped, like an out-of-control Amtrak toward the rotten bridge that marked a quarter of a century of living on earth. *A quarter. Of. A century.*

There she met Grayson, an exceedingly mellow guy with waist-length usually unwashed animal-cracker-brown hair, a cool beatnikish crook in his neck, tummy muscles taut as the rubber skin on a trampoline, and a monosyllabic vocabulary. As well as this large stash of ecstasy, which candy lured her into this near-stranger's apartment late one night (or actually early one morning) after this totally awesome moshing session at Club Foot, and then sent her scrambling into the gray-and-brick streets at six a.m. (without the benefit of her army-surplus jacket) under a dangerously low winter sky when she awoke with this distinct impression she had just performed sex with Mr. Death himself only to discover an unused condom on the pillow by her head and a couple of bloody fingerprints on the nearby off-white wall. At which point (remembering too godawfully well the nightmarish day she'd learned from Flynn that he'd been simultaneously boffing the underfed bassist for Blackwater Scabies named Renna, the cheesy-skinned mutant of a waitress at the local IHOP named Lida, and the Venus-of-Willendorf-chested groupy with those myriad haunting coldsores named Pia: "Hey," he'd said, "if it bothers you so much I'll quit") she swore off human relationships all together, cold turkey, opting instead for the kind of concentrated and single-minded celibacy that a Buddhist monk might honestly envy, and plunged head-long into her new series of triptychs, as well as into this addictive virtual community of down-and-outers not un-like herself she uncovered on this subversive chat space based somewhere in British Columbia that Grayson had introduced her to just before he scared himself right out of the picture.

It was called Mansion of the Maniacal Mesons, or M^3 for short, and it worked like this. You read a little neatly fonted paragraph sliding down your screen about the pros and cons (but mostly pros) of anarchy, chaos, and general decenteredness in the cosmos, and then through a series of virtual directions entered various virtual rooms in the vir-tual mansion dedicated to various virtual bizarrenesses. In one environment, for instance, you could talk to people committed to building a tactical nuclear device which would then be used to bully governments around the world into peace. In another, you could exchange ideas with folks who maintained that the human species had for all intents and purposes run its course and that someday the planet would be inhabited by artificial intelligences that viewed humans as a necessary if messy rung on the laborious lad-der of evolution. And in yet another you could gossip with a tribe who dubbed themselves Paranoids Anonymous and maintained that the universe was just one vast conspiracy aimed against none other than the PA system itself, the JFK assassination only the most commonly cited example, but others including everything from the spread of AIDS to the choice of Superfund sites, the apparent smart drugs hoax to the inorganic compounds used in certain brands of fertilizer, the Jesse Ventura candidacy to the multifoliate cover-ups involved with this and that southwestern UFO visitation.

Alexis, however, always returned to the Cybersex Cell. Here people with such monikers as French Kiss, Blowtorch, and Whiplash congregated and carried on conversations that would probably sometimes make Linda Lovelace blush if she'd been privy to them. The CC was a dazzlingly dark and kinky space that often caught Alexis's breath in her throat, widened her eyes, made her body sink back in her chair in astonishment, not because of the rampantly uncommon obscenities that transpired there, jeez no, although there were plenty of those, but because of the sheer *force* of creativity, honesty, and the ability on Alexis's part to become anyone she wanted at the click of an ENTER key, someone she couldn't be anywhere else in the whole world, to slip on alternate identities in the same way another might slip on a negligee, or maybe a really nice pair of pre-washed 501's—and do so as safely as if she were taking a little after-dinner stroll through a silly set from Sesame Street which, in a cybernetic sense, was just what she was doing.

And so one night, a handful of snowy feathers bobbing outside her window among a cubist painting of warehouse roofs, Alexis became Digital Matrix as easily as Clark Kent became Superman. Her Mac was her phonebooth, her keyboard her cape. She grew to be the five-ten she'd always wanted to be. She dyed her hair in ten-minute intervals, spiking it spider-black, razoring it down to pumpkin-orange fuzz, cultivating it into a long pistachio-green or yolk-yellow tress that tickled all the way to the muscled curves of her buttocks. She tattooed a bloodshot eyeball onto her left shoulder blade, an emerald-and-blue planet onto the back of her neck, a fat golden phallic cobra (hood distended, fangs dripping venom) winding up her right leg, and she donned a tight leather flightsuit, silver-and-black platform boots, glossy crimson nail polish, diamond tongue-stud, three nose rings, cartoon treasure chest of hoops and bracelets and necklaces. She spoke in a husky voice, became bright and bold and sassily ironic, smoked the occasional unfiltered cigarette, changed her eye-color from breadmold gray to methyl violet, no, Wedgwood blue, no, café-noir brown, and, as a final present to herself, uncovered a mysterious and complex ancestry that fed her features, replaced her bland blond-leading-the-blond Midwestern one, and included some royal Eastern European genes, a couple of very pure German ones, and, needless to say, a healthy ninjaed dose of Japanese. Before long she was spending two, three hours a night at her console, mostly teasing compu-nerds across north America who were, it seemed, pretty much lining up to fantasize with Alexis. Until, that is, she jacked into her Mac one particularly cold evening, remnants of a dry Domino's pizza (predictable veggie combo) crinkled and curled in its box on the table beside her keyboard.

LUST IN THE MATRIX (1)

DIGITAL MATRIX TELEPORTS IN, SAYS, "yo, dOOds, someone ready to sMoke? ;)"
ERIC WAVES, SAYS, "Hi."
DIGITAL MATRIX, ASTOUNDED, SAYS, "*hi*? *Hi*?"
ERIC SAYS, "yeah, well. prtty nEw at this sorT a th ing. Um, YO."
DIGITAL MATRIX SLAPPING HER FOREHEAD, RUBBING HER HANDS IN GLEE.
ERIC SAYS, "sorry. ill, um, just slink away right now"
DIGITAL MATRIX SAYS, "dont you *dare.* Come to momma, little boy."
ERIC APPROACHES, SAYS, "just cheCking things out."

DIGITAL MATRIX ASKS, "Cherry to the cybersex cell?"
ERIC RESPONDS, "cherry to the mansion."
DIGITAL MATRIX ASKS, "where u from?"
ERIC SAYS, "seattle."
DIGITAL MATRIX SAYS, "really? Me too. In a manner
of speaking. what u do?"
ERIC ANSWERS, "student."
DIGITAL MATRIX ASKS, "ahat kind?"
ERIC RESPONDS, "hischool."
DIGITAL MATRIX DISPLAYS MUCH RUBBING OF
HANDS AND GNASHING OF TEETH.
DIGITAL MATRIX ASKS, "what u wearing tonight?"
ERIC RESPONDS, "stuff jeans tshirt sneakers Y?"
DIGITAL MATRIX GASPS, "!!!!!!!!!!"
ERIC SAYS, "oh I get it make something up"
DIGITAL MATRIX SAYS, "my poor poor little boy"
ERIC SCRATCHES HIS HEAD, SAYS, "Ok lez see now
..."
DIGITAL MATRIX SAYS, "i smell a tutorial here. The
scent is powerful ..."
ERIC SAYS, "Sounds gOod. w hen do we begin?"
DIGITAL MATRIX SAYS, "bring your seatbelt tonight?"
ERIC SAYS, "buckling up even as we speak"
DIGITAL MATRIX SAYS, "so much to learn and so little
time"

DIGITAL MATRIX ASKS, "Eric, sweet thing, you with
me?"

DIGITAL MATRIX SAYS, "hello?"

ERIC SAYS, "gotta go. DAd needs to use the computer
talk to ya soon"

DIGITAL MATRIX SAYS, "*Dad*?"

DIGITAL MATRIX SAYS, "*Dad*?"

DIGITAL MATRIX SHRUGS AND LEVITATES TO-
WARD THE CYBERWINGS.

@QUIT

DIGITAL MATRIX TELEPORTS IN, ASKS, "Eric, you
out there this evening, honey?"
ERIC SAYS, "over here. hoping youd show."
DIGITAL MATRIX SAYS, "good to see ya"
ERIC ASKS, "wAnna know what i m wearing?"
DIGITAL MATRIX SMILES, TONGUE-STUD FLASH-
ING.
DIGITAL MATRIX SAYS, "fast learner i'm all ears."
ERIC SAYS, "black code west boots levis turtleneck
mirrorshades."
DIGITAL MATRIX RESPONDS, "gOl star"
ERIC DISPLAYS MUCH BLUSHING AND DIGGING
OF BOOT-TOES INTO THE VIRTUAL SAND.
ERIC SAYS, ";-)"
DIGITAL MATRIX ASKS, "so u live in seattle?"
ERIC ANSWERS, "near uw can see uinion bay from my
bedroom window you?"
DIGITAL MATRIX SAYS, "block off e Madison tellme
bout eric."
ERIC SAYS, "17. fAst learner. got these theories"
DIGITAL MATRIX ASKS, "such as"
ERIC SAYS, "ever get the impression things are like
speeding up"
DIGITAL MATRIX SAYS, "things?"
ERIC SAYS, "the city the world everything like you turn
on the news at 6 ..."
DIGITAL MATRIX SAYS, "... ?"
ERIC SAYS, "an its completely diffrent from what u saw
at 5"
DIGITAL MATRIX SAYS, "You got my attention."
ERIC SAYS, "song #1 last month?"

DIGITAL MATRIX SAYS, "… ?"
ERIC SAYS, "when u hear it again u cant remember if u heard it befor"
DIGITAL MATRIX SAYS, "like you only dimly recollect it from when you were 7."
ERIC SAYS, "an if this is the future were living in … "
DIGITAL MATRIX SAYS, "then wHat could possbly come next?"
ERIC SAYS, "its like amazingly hard to remember what day it is"
DIGITAL MATRIX SAYS, "rr what you di yesterday."
ERIC SAYS, "and day before that is just out of the question"
DIGITAL MATRIX SAYS, "like 500000000000 bc"
ERIC SAYS, "tomorrow …"
DIGITAL MATRIX SAYS, "Oof, tomorrow …"

CHAOS THEORY

"Far from being a bad or a negative thing, chaos is a positive aspect of the world, expressing the beautiful diversity of phenomena as well as the underlying cosmic rhythms. The fact that the world is an incompressibly complex chaotic computation means that there is no way to predict the future other than physically living through the time it takes to get there. Surprise is always possible, and a state of chaos is a state of health." —Rudy Rucker

"If your brain software is on the disc, the computer can simulate you, and you will be, in some sense, alive inside the computer." —Rudy Rucker

"I think that if you *could* become a cyborg for reasons of intellectual ecstasy, one day you'd discover that you've passed out in the street, and there are roaches living in your artificial arm." —Bruce Sterling

LUST IN THE MATRIX (2)

ERIC ASKS, "know what i think"
DIGITAL MATRIX RESPONDS, "… ?"
ERIC SAYS, "were all a lot more conservative than we pretend we r"
DIGITAL MATRIX SAYS, "as in we live this way not cuz we want to"
ERIC SAYS, "but cuz we have to   deep in our hearts"
DIGITAL MATRIX SAYS, "deep in our hearts we all want to appear on mtv."
ERIC SAYS, "deep in our hearts we all want to be a different target market"

LUST IN THE MATRIX (3)

DIGITAL MATRIX SAYS, "and what will our jobs look like when werre 35?"
ERIC ANSWERS, "we ll need to get used to a little less every day my father claims no worthwhile males were born after 1966"
DIGITAL MATRIX ASKS, "… ?"
ERIC SAYS, "thre already too comfortable wiT the idea of failure"
DIGITAL MATRIX SAYS, "children of the 60s"
ERIC SAYS, "flower children"
DIGITAL MATRIX SAYS, "freudian nightmares"

ERIC SAYS, "no motivation no ambition deepseeded belief in fate"
DIGITAL MATRIX ASKS, "And u?"
ERIC SAYS, "hard parts knowing secretly the guy may just have this point"
DIGITAL MATRIX SAYS, "waz your mom say?"
ERIC RESPONDS, "she lives in san francisco sensnce I was 5 mom renamed herself after a season"
DIGITAL MATRIX CONSOLES, "i'm so so sorry."
ERIC SAYS, "she believes in berries reincarnation timophy weary. my father renamed himself after a motorcycle."
DIGITAL MATRIX SAYS, "he didt."
ERIC SAYS, "harley d. i'm so existentially embarrassed."
DIGITAL MATRIX SAYS, "i'm history ... but then arent we all?"

LUST IN THE MATRIX (4)

ERIC SAYS, "u live off east madson?"
DIGITAL MATRIX SAYS, "moved in couple mOnths ago"
ERIC ASKS, "how come?"
DIGITAL MATRIX SAYS, "ya don wanna knowx"
ERIC SAYS, "i do."
DIGITAL MATRIX SAYS, "guy prob"
ERIC SAYS, "*You?*"
DIGITAL MATRIX SAYS, "my life isnt holly consisent with my media imagea"
ERIC SAYS, "u give us all reason to hope"
DIGITAL MATRIX SAYS, "I seem to attract guys your dad was talking about."
ERIC SAYS, "Tell me."
DIGITAL MATRIX ASKS, "You really want to know? here goes. i was living with this guy."
ERIC SAYS, "musician, right?"

DIGITAL MATRIX ASKS, "howed u know that?"
ERIC SAYS, "at some level you really loved him"
DIGITAL MATRIX SAYS, "cant even begin to tell you
how much only"
ERIC SAYS, "only he was a real asshole"
DIGITAL MATRIX SAYS, "selfabsrbed lazy messy some-
times cruel in a really just osrt of weirdly unconscious
wya"
ERIC SAYS, "an really really talented"
DIGITAL MATRIX SAYS, "and really really talented."
ERIC SAYS, "one of those things it should have worked
out in the future."
DIGITAL MATRIX SAYS, "Only the future never ar-
rived."
ERIC SAYS, "only somewhere way down deep you think
maybe it still might"
DIGITAL MATRIX ASKS, "So what ya wearin tonight?"
ERIC RESPONDS, "black code west boots levis turtle-
neck mirrorshades"
DIGITAL MATRIX SAYS, "no i mean really"
ERIC SAYS, "hey no fair."
DIGITAL MATRIX SAYS, "… ?"
ERIC ANSWERS, "jean black tshirt sneakers"

ERIC ASKS, "hey uu with me"

DIGITAL MATRIX SAYS, "tak em off"

ERIC SAYS, "???"
DIGITAL MATRIX SAYS, "u heard me go on"
ERIC SAYS, "as in realy"
DIGITAL MATRIX SAYS, "as in do it"

ERIC SAYS, "dun"
DIGITAL MATRIX SAYS, "ok jus a sec"

DIGITAL MATRIX SAYS, "so tell me what your doing
right now"

ERIC ANSWERS, "sitting in my bed powerbook in lap its dark"
DIGITAL MATRIX SAYS, "cept for the glow from the screen"
ERIC SAYS, "right"
DIGITAL MATRIX ASKS, "dadd asleep?"
ERIC RESPONDS, "dead to the world. U?"
DIGITAL MATRIX SAYS, "at my desk next to my window lights off looking out"
ERIC ASKS, "what u see?"
DIGITAL MATRIX SAYS, "lonely city puddle on roof pink sky"
ERIC SAYS, "sounds sad"
DIGITAL MATRIX SAYS, "only i'm not in my apartment anymore."
ERIC SAYS, "u're not?"
DIGITAL MATRIX SAYS, "i'm in your bed eric putting your computer aside"
ERIC SAYS, "o'm runnjng my fingers througr your hair"
DIGITAL MATRIX SAYS, "straddling your lap reaching down hands warm"
ERIC SAYS, "i can feel it"
DIGITAL MATRIX SAYS, "i'm squeezing thumbing the tip"
ERIC SAYS, "reaching for your breats"
DIGITAL MATRIX SAYS, "nipples erect"
ERIC SAYS, "barely touching them with my tonge"
DIGITAL MATRIX SAYS, "mmmmmmm just like that i'm easing down"
ERIC SAYS, "and we can hear my dad in the next room"
DIGITAL MATRIX SAYS, "we're rocking real gently sofly"
ERIC SAYS, "he cant hear us"
DIGITAL MATRIX SAYS, "but were colonizing his dreams"

SEATTLE:KEN:ALPHA

And so they made a date to interface two noons hence at the Naked Lunch, this cute little new red-and-white-table-cloth-with-candle café Alexis recently began to frequent in Capitol Hill because, they figured, it was time to meet on the grainy gray-and-brick streets of Seattle in the gritty Big Room. Because, Alexis knew, she had finally found (teetering on the very abysmal brink of her twenty-third year, not more than three months after swallowing the sour fact that she'd never find anyone with whom to feel anything save that she was talking French while he gobbled and clucked some version of Malayo-Polynesian) a sensitive, smart, and thoughtful guy who understood things the same way she understood them, felt things the very same way she felt them, as if the traffic lights on the corner of East Madison and Broadway had abruptly changed and they'd just stepped off the curb at the exact same second. This wasn't, she told herself as she tried to work on her new series of triptychs, and discovered she couldn't, obsessed as she was about what to wear (it had to be casual yet suave, hip yet fashionably non-threatening, black but not *too* black), and came up empty-closeted, something about the hoped-for future. No. Not at all. This wasn't the abstract ether of the subjunctive, but the cold hard cash of the declarative. This was, she told herself as she tugged on her black tights and baggy black boxers, tied her maroon hightops with the dark green laces and clicked in place her matching choker, fastened her gaudy rhinestone earrings and puffed up her huge, floppy, maroon-and-olive-striped Cat-in-the-Hat hat atop her head, the bedrock on which to build an earthquake-proof edifice of safety, good feelings, and longevity. This was *it*, finally it, she told herself as she sat fiddling with her menu at the Naked Lunch, the moment of truth, cup of cappuccino steaming before her, the instant of enlightenment, twilit Saturday noontime shading the street beyond the picture-window into violets and pearls...at five past the hour, at seven, at twelve, at fifteen, her chemicals sizzling through her heart like so many luminous radioactive isotopes, her cliff-hanging apprehension equaled only by the big galoot of fear scratching its armpits and drumming its hairy finger stumps on the table beside her, breath a week-old morass of potential failure and loss—until, that is, that sugary, reflexive, plaque-filled smile buoyed up through the small sea of masticating mouths, artificial laughter, and burping babies, one of the most genuinely vulnerable and bewildered grins on a five-o'clock-shadowed deliverer-of-cigarettes-to-various-vending-machines-around-town face you are ever likely to see, and the firm fast realization swept across Alexis's consciousness that this is how it would always work itself out, every time, pieces snapping into place when it no longer mattered whether they did or not, as Flynn pulled up a rickety chair opposite her, slouched into it, and waved at the approaching waitress for service, marrow-knocking whiff of patchouli in the air, while Alexis comprehended the concept of serendipity for the first instant in her life, *really* comprehended it, kismet, karma, providence, the way she had by chance been duped by a twenty-two-year-old musician and slacker in the warm gray glow of the matrix—and she sighed and leaned back in her own chair, a little less rickety than Flynn's, a wide, glimmering, affectionate smile spreading across her lips like hope itself.

Because she understood that *this* was as happy as she would ever be, right here, right now, it would get no better, and so she wanted only one thing, really, longed for only one accomplishment: to savor its genuine sweetness and light till that moment in ten minutes or ten years when she would stand and walk out once more.

X-Ray Dreams, 1963

Daddy Grilling, His Head a TV Set
The dream won't stop arriving. Every night. At the office, too. In the evenings with Mother & Uncle Billy & Panzer after dinner watching "My Three Sons." In the dream, I have a golden doughnut. Sometimes it's called the garden, sometimes a hair pie, sometimes where the monkey sleeps. But it's always the same. It's always there, mulberry moist & swollen. It's always a miracle, like trying to imagine what comes after time & space. I spend hours investigating, palpating lightly as milkweed umbels, sliding in my middle finger, thumb & forefinger & middle finger, whole hand, arm to elbow, extracting a wedding garter, an invisible cat that won't quit purring, three pennies, a 1927 Babe Ruth baseball card, an orb of light with iridescent bluebird wings. Then I feel someone tapping my forehead & open my eyes to magpies making bloody jam of my frontal lobes.

Uncle Billy in a Dress, Daydreaming

Oh!—it's simply the most beautiful thing, isn't it, *dobos*-torte
sweet knowledge, because you can feel it underneath your
smart dress & know it's always there…when you're eat-
ing, say, or when you're talking to the postman, unfolding
the Castro Convertible for well-behaved guests, pouring a
cup of new & improved Tide into the washing machine,
because you know it's there & that's the most indescrib-
ably stunning thing, it makes you feel free to know, no
matter what you're doing, vacuuming or head lowered
Sunday morning, because its existence proves everything
will be absolutely scrumptious, & I could stand up & dance,
stand up & gambol this very minute, like Julie Andrews
across the Alpine meadow, hair cropped short as mine,
black-&-white dress a-billow like a penguin in billowing
grass, arms stretched wide to the ambient possibility of
music & to Disney executives at mahogany tables everywhere because, well, because I know I happen to look drop-
dead gorgeous tonight in my carefully plucked eyebrows
& tasteful, understated brooch that would make Jackie O.
proud, neat as a just-turned-down bed: I could stand &
dance while Nancy sweeps up her Kodak to capture this
rich moment to share with the future, no matter what Rob-
ert is opening his filthy mouth to say, thinking you can't
see it but you can, opening his mouth to say across the room,
lips parting, because what he says he says from darkhearted
jealousy, never able to look as dreamboat perfect as me here,
tonight, my spectacular secret alive between my meticu-
lously shaven legs.

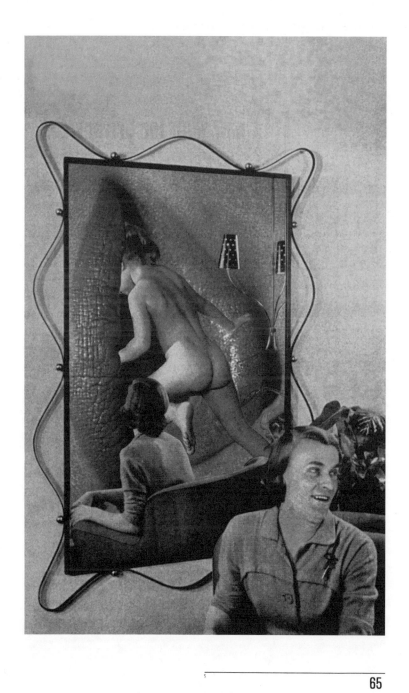

Mother Gagged in the Family Room

Commentary

The Clitoris is situated beneath the anterior commissure, partially hidden between the anterior extremities of the labia minora. The body is short and concealed beneath the labia; the free extremity, or *glans clitoridis*, is a small rounded tubercle, consisting of spongy erectile tissue, and highly sensitive. It is provided, like the penis, with a suspensory ligament. The clitoris consists of two corpora cavernosa, composed of erectile tissue enclosed in a dense layer of fibrous membrane, united by an incomplete fibrous pectiniform septum.

The Penis consists of a root, body, and highly sensitive extremity, the *glans penis*. It is composed, like the clitoris, of a mass of erectile tissue, and enclosed in three cylindrical fibrous compartments. Two, the corpora cavernosa, are placed side by side along the upper part of the organ; the third, or corpus spongiosum, encloses the urethra and is placed below. The septum between these is thick and complete behind, incomplete in front, and consists of vertical bands arranged like the teeth of a comb [L. *pecten, -inis*, comb, scallop].

Mother's Hunchbacked Reflection, Daydreaming
The dream won't stop arriving. Every night. Running errands, too. In the evenings with Father & Uncle Billy & Panzer after dinner watching "The Donna Reed Show." In the dream, there is a cobblestone town square. The sky is chilly gray. A crowd has gathered to watch six clowns perform. The clowns ride unicycles while doing handstands. Play an accordion with their feet. Juggle flaming bowling pins. The crowd applauds. Afterwards, the clowns move among the onlookers with a shabby tophat, collecting. When they reach a group of small children standing in front of their festive parents, they proffer the hat. The children, thinking the goods inside are theirs, plunge their hands in. One pulls out, not the spare change people have been depositing, but a white rabbit in wire-rimmed glasses. Everyone cheers. The clowns simper & proffer the children the hat again. Dazzled, the children thrust in their hands & this time one extracts a huge, colorful, paper-flower bouquet. The crowd erupts in admiration. When the clowns proffer the children the hat a third time, the children, giggling & sputtering with merriment, jab in their hands &, next, one is holding a giant glistening purple-red clitoris with wet floppy labia. The crowd, baffled, goes still. The children open their mouths to scream. But just then the giant sex bird begins flapping its fleshy wings, rising out of the astonished child's palm, circling over the heads of the onlookers & then higher & higher over the town square, above the medieval rooftops, into the chilly gray sky, until it is a moist liver, until it is a black dot, until it is nothing at all.

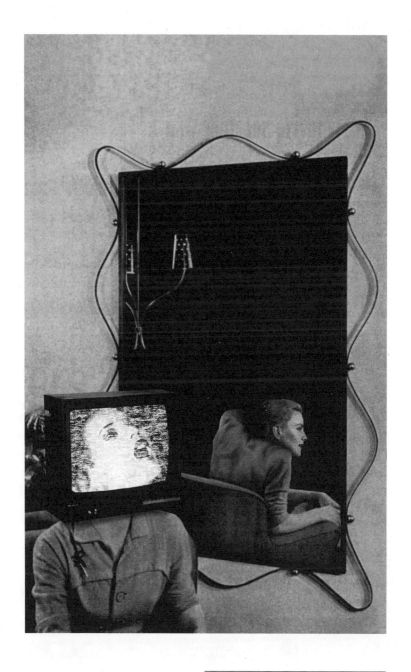

Panzer Playing, Her Head a TV Set

I am the person who becomes you, like it or not. I am the person whom you can never become again. I am the person you can look at from the outside but never really understand. Knowing this cuts up your heart at least once every day, often when you least expect it, riding the subway home after work, opening the refrigerator door & reaching for a pint of ice cream. I am the person who recites the dreams my parents never had. I am the person who sticks so many thoughts into my uncle's mind that his mind in the end becomes my mind. Because I had a sister who used to beat me, kick me off swings, clip my hair with gardening shears while I cried. Because my name isn't Panzer. Because it never was. Because my father wouldn't listen when I told him, over & over, & my mother said I'd have been a better person if I hadn't been adopted. Because freaks are just like humans, only more so. Because one day when I was four, playing with my dolls in the family room, I somehow didn't realize that 34 years later I would dream that I looked down at my arm & saw something slithering around underneath the skin, a little hard pea that reminded me of PacMan, & I began to scratch at it but it wouldn't stop so I became terrified that beetles called the past were living in me subdermally, only then the skin over my right carpal tunnel unfolded like a fastforward orchid & a supernumerary clitoris surfaced & I gave it to my husband & he lay it on his tongue & played with it, nibbling & licking, for hours, & then he slipped it down his pants, & I grasped that everything was going to work out okay in the end.

Cybermorphic
Beat-Up Get-Down
Subterranean Homesick
Reality-Sandwich Blues

I'm a, like, poet. Mona. Mona Sausalito. I write lyrics for my boyfriend's band, Plato's Deathmetal Tumors. Plato's Deathmetal Tumors kicks butt. It's one of the best Neogoth bands in Seattle. My boyfriend's name is Mosh. Mosh shaved his head and tattooed it with rad circuitry patterns. He plays wicked cool lead and sings like Steve Tyler on amphetamines. Only that's not his real name. His real name is Marvin Goldstein. But so. Like I say, I'm a poet. I write about human sacrifices, cannibalism, vampires, and stuff. Mosh loves my work. He says we're all going to be famous some day. Only right now we're not, which bites, cuz I've been writing for like almost ten months. These things take time, I guess. Except we need some, like, cash to get by from week to week? Which is why Mosh one day says take the job at Escort à la Mode. Why not? I say. Which I guess kind of brings me to my story.

See, I'm cruising Capitol Hill in one of the company's black BMWs when my car-phone rings. Escort à la Mode's a real high-class operation. Escortettes' services go for $750 an hour. We usually work with foreign business types. Japs

and ragheads mostly. Politicians, too. With 24 hours' notice, we can also supply bogus daughters, brothers, and
sons. You name it. Except there's absolutely nothing kinky
here. We don't even kiss the clients. No way. Handshakes
max. Take them out, show them the town, eat at a nice restaurant, listen to them yak, take them to a club, watch them
try to dance, take them home. Period. We're tour guides,
like. Our goal is to make people feel interesting. Therma
Payne—she's my boss—Therma says our job is to "give
good consort." Therma's a scream.

But so. Like I say, my car-phone rings. I answer. Dis-
patcher gives me an address, real chi-chi bookstore called
Hard Covers down by the fish market. My client's supposed
to be this big-deal writer guy who's reading there. Poet.
Supposed to've been famous back in like the Pleistocene
Error or something. So important I never even heard of him.
But, hey. It's work.

Now I'm not being like unmodest or anything, okay?
But I happen to be fricking gorgeous. No shit. My skin's
real white. I dye my hair, which is short and spiked, shoe-
polish black, then streak it with these little wisps of pink.
Which picks up my Lancôme Corvette-red lipstick and long
Estée Lauder Too-Good-To-Be-Natural black lashes. When
I talk with a client, I'll keep my eyes open real wide so I
always look Winona-Ryder-surprised by what he's saying.
I'm 5'2", and when I wear my Number Four black-knit
body-dress and glossy black Mouche army boots I become
every middle-aged man's bad-little-girl wetdream. So I
don't just *walk* in to Hard Covers, okay? I kind of, what,
sashay. Yeah. That's it. *Sashay*. I've never been there before,
and I'm frankly pretty fucking impressed. Place is just
humongous. More a warehouse than a bookstore. Except that
it's all mahogany and bronze and dense carpeting. Health-
food bar. Espresso counter. Dweeb with bat-wing ears playing muzak at the baby grand. Area off on the side with a
podium and loads of chairs for the reading. Which is already filling. Standing room only. People are real excited.

And books. God. Books. Enough books to make you instantly anxious you'll never read them all, no way, no matter how hard you try, so you mind as well not.

I'm right on time. So I ask the guy at the register for the famous rich poet. He points to the storeroom. Warming up, he says. So I go on back and knock, only no one answers. I knock again. Nada. My meter's running, and I figure I mind as well earn my paycheck, so I try the knob. Door's unlocked. I open it, stick my head in, say hi. It's pretty dark, all shadows and book cartons, and the room stretches on forever, and I'm already getting bored, so I enter and close the door behind me. When my eyes adjust a little, I make out a dim light way off in a distant corner. I start weaving toward it through the rows and rows of cartons. As I get closer, I can hear these voices. They sound kind of funny. Worried, like. Real fast and low. And then I see them. I see the whole thing.

Maybe five or six guys in gray business suits and ties, real like FBI or something, are huddling over this jumble on the floor. At first I don't understand what I'm looking at. Then I make out the portable gurney. And this torso on it, just this torso, naked and fleshy pink in a doll sort of way, rib cage big as a cow's, biggest fucking belly you ever saw. Out of it are sticking these skinny white flabby legs, between them this amazingly small little purple dick and two hairy marbles. Only, thing is, the chest isn't a real chest? There's a panel in it. And the panel's open. And one of the guys is tinkering with some wiring in there. And another is rummaging through a wooden crate, coming up with an arm, plugging it into the torso, while a third guy, who's been balancing a second arm over his shoulder like a rifle or something, swings it down and locks it into place.

I may be a poet, okay, but I'm not a fucking liar or anything. I'm just telling you what I saw. Believe it or not. Go ahead. Frankly I don't give a shit. But I'm telling you, I'm standing there, hypnotized like, not sure whether to run or wet myself, when this fourth guy reaches into the crate and comes up with, I kid you not, the *head*. I swear. I fucking swear. A *head*. The thing is so gross. Pudgy. Bushy. Gray-haired. And with these *eyes*. With these sort of glazed *eyes* that're looking up into the darkness where the ceiling should've been. I could hurl just thinking about it.

Anyway, after a pretty long time fidgeting with the stuff in the chest, they prop the torso into a sitting position and start attaching the head. It's not an easy job. They fiddle and curse, and once one of them slips with a screwdriver and punctures the thing's left cheek. Only they take some flesh-toned silicon putty junk and fill up the hole, which works just fine. And the third guy reaches into his breast pocket and produces these wire-rimmed glasses, which he slips into place on the thing's face, and then they stand back, arms folded, admiring their work and all, and then the first guy reaches behind the thing's neck and pushes what must've been the ON/OFF button.

Those eyes roll down and snap into focus. Head swivels side to side. Mouth opens and closes its fatty lips, testing. And then, shit, it begins *talking*. It begins fucking *talking*.

I'm with you in Rockland. I'm wuh-wuh-wuh-with you...But my agent. What sort of agent is that? What could she have been thinking? Have you seen those sales figures? A stone should have better figures than that! I'm wuh-with you in the nightmare of trade paperbacks, sudden flash of bad PR, suffering the outrageousness of weak blurbs and failing shares. Where is the breakthrough book? Where the advance? Share with me the vanity of the unsolicited manuscript! Show me the madman bum of a publicist! Movie rights! Warranties! Indemnities! I am the twelve percent royalty! I am the first five-thousand copies! I am the retail and the wholesale, the overhead and the option clause! Give me the bottom line! Give me the tax break! Give me a reason to collect my rough drafts in the antennae crown of commerce! Oh, mental, mental, mental hardcover! Oh, incomplete clause! Oh, hopeless abandon of the unfulfilled contract! I am wuh-wuh-wuh-with you...I am wuh-wuh-wuh-with you in Rockland...I am...

"Oh, shit," says the first guy.

"Balls," says the second.

"We should've let him go," says the third guy.

"When his ticker stopped," says the first.

"When his liver quit," says the second.

"One thing," says the fourth. "Nanotech sure ain't what it's cracked up to be."

"You got that right," says the third.

Thirty thousand books in 1998 alone, the famous rich poet says, *but they couldn't afford it. Tangier, Venice, Amsterdam. What were they thinking? Wall Street is holy! The New York Stock Exchange is holy! The cosmic clause is holy! I'm wuh-wuh-wuh...I'm wuh-wuh-wuh...wuh-wuh-wuh...*

"Turn him off," says the fifth one.

Pale greenish foam begins forming on the famous rich poet's lips, dribbling down his chin, spattering his hairless chest.

"Yeah, well," says the second.

"Guess we got some tightening to do," says the third, reaching behind the thing's neck.

But just as he pressed that button, just for a fraction of an instant, the stare of the famous rich poet fell on me as I tried scrunching out of sight behind a wall of boxes. Our eyes met. His looked like those of a wrongly convicted murderer maybe like one second before the executioner throws the switch that'll send a quadrillion volts zizzing through his system. In them was this mixture of disillusionment, dismay, fear, and uninterrupted sorrow. I froze. He stretched his foam-filled mouth as wide as it would go, ready to bellow, ready to howl. Except the juice failed. His mouth slowly closed again. His eyes rolled back up inside his head.

And me?

I said fuck this. Fuck the books, fuck the suits, fuck Escort à la Mode, fuck the withered old pathetic shit. This whole thing's *way* too fricking rich for *my* blood.

And so I turned and walked.

SEWING SHUT MY EYES

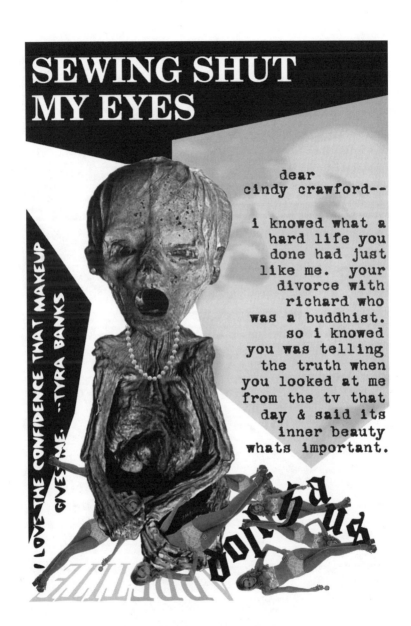

I LOVE THE CONFIDENCE THAT MAKEUP GIVES ME. --TYRA BANKS

dear
cindy crawford--

i knowed what a
hard life you
done had just
like me. your
divorce with
richard who
was a buddhist.
so i knowed
you was telling
the truth when
you looked at me
from the tv that
day & said its
inner beauty
whats important.

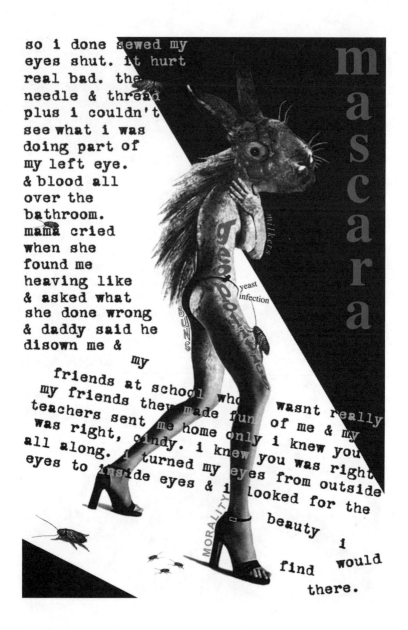

so i done sewed my
eyes shut. it hurt
real bad. the
needle & thread
plus i couldn't
see what i was
doing part of
my left eye.
& blood all
over the
bathroom.
mama cried
when she
found me
heaving like
& asked what
she done wrong
& daddy said he
disown me &
            my
    friends at school who   wasnt really
   my friends they made fun of me & my
  teachers sent   me home only i knew you
  was right, cindy. i knew you was right
 all along. i turned my eyes from outside
 eyes to inside eyes & i looked for the
                        beauty
                               i
                   find   would
                        there.

mascara

milkers

yeast
infection

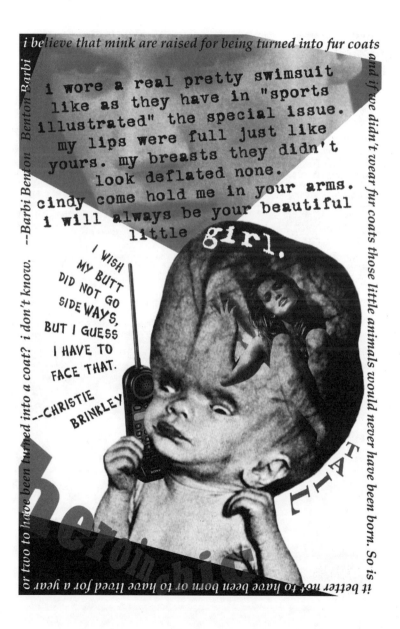

i believe that mink are raised for being turned into fur coats

i wore a real pretty swimsuit like as they have in "sports illustrated" the special issue. my lips were full just like yours. my breasts they didn't look deflated none. cindy come hold me in your arms. i will always be your beautiful little girl.

--Barbi Benton Benton Barbi

I WISH MY BUTT DID NOT GO SIDEWAYS, BUT I GUESS I HAVE TO FACE THAT.

--CHRISTIE BRINKLEY

and if we didn't wear fur coats those little animals would never have been born. So is

it better not to have been born or to have lived for a year or two to have been turned into a coat? i don't know.

everyone everywhere looked just like me.

i was so

I tried on 250 bathing suits in one afternoon and ended up having little scabs up and down my thighs, probably from some of those with sequins all over them.
2. Cindy Crawford

I don't wake up for less than $10,000.00 a day.
1. Linda Evangelista

happy.

NO HUMAN FEMALE COULD PHYSICALLY ENDURE ACTUAL EMBODIMENT IN BARBIE'S ULTRA-SLIM PROPORTIONS. HER BONES WOULD BE TOO THIN AND BRITTLE, THE FORCE OF GRAVITY TOO STRONG. NOT TO MENTION THE UNBEARABLE AGONY OF ELONGATION, EMACIATING . . .
—STEVE SHAVIRO

INSTANT

when the doc cut open my eyes all i could see was

VENGEANCE

television sets, your face.

Once, when my mother mentioned an amount and I realized I didn't understand, she had to explain that's like three Mercedes. Then I understood.

3. Brooke Shields

Kamikaze Motives
of the Immaculate Deconstruction
in the Data-Sucking Rust-Age
of Insectile Hackers

They sent down the robotic cockroaches first. Back in the eighties. To Wall Street, mainly, though they also hit Beijing and Moscow. The evidence is overwhelming. It was all recon, checking things out, the intergalactic shock troops, with insects that looked just like all the other insects around them—the ones under that metal chair in the corner of the Stock Exchange, the ones under the sheaf of papers in that filing cabinet in Red Square—unless you picked them up, unless you examined them real close. Cuz then you saw, if you squinted, the cameras just behind those dark polymer eye shells.

You think I don't know how that sounds? You think I don't know you want to treat me like one of those kids born without noses? Well, don't. Cuz it's true. All of it's true. Every single word.

I'm the Raz, the Fed, the one They never told you about. I do the jobs that don't exist. I investigate the incidents that never happened. And this is my report from the front. This is my last dispatch. I'm sitting in the bedroom on the second floor of our safe house in East LA, Yeltsin-70 in one hand and cassette in the other, and they're on the stairs, man, they're coming up. So here goes. This is it. This is how it ends.

They sent in the robotic cockroaches first. No one noticed. They went about their business, collecting data, organizing details, sniffing air, chewing detritus they chanced on. Recording. They were droids, cosmic notation instruments, with nano hard-drives for heads and vacuum cleaners for stomachs and assorted monitors for antennae. They gathered information like other insects gathered pheromones and food, continuously, relentlessly, sampling the temperature, UV emissions, background radiation, skittering into the national mainframes and hacking the codes, burning the neural networks of the globe, downloading the digital identity that made the planet itself. They discovered how governments functioned, how the hive-mind of the media performed. They ascertained our economic machinery, our technical acumen, the geography of our corporate imaginations.

Then they started going for the tissue samples. They infiltrated the hospitals, harvesting. They took epidermal clippings from sleeping patients. Accumulated drug specimens from the pharmacies. Impervious to cold, they invaded the icy nightmare-crypts of the morgues, burrowing deep through tympanic membrane, incus, cochlea, vestibular nerve, directly into the brain.

Which is where the first one was exposed in the fall of 1989 by an autopsist during a routine postmortem on a burst parietal aneurysm at the Columbia Medical Center in New York. Nesting among the semisolid gel, the thing—flat slippery body housed in a leathery yellow-brown casing, bristly legs, flickering feelers—hissed at her when she uncovered it. The autopsist, Dr. Fiona K'ai-chih, removed the orthopteron with tweezers and crushed its armored head. Instead of umber sap, a demure blue spark flittered out. Dr. K'ai-chih slipped the carcass under a microscope and saw, behind what was left of those dark polymer eye shells, the cameras. She called the police. The police called the FBI. The FBI called the CIA. And the CIA called us.

I entered the narrative in August, 1990, after way too much had already gone down. I was there, really, to bear witness. I was there for the metaphorical dustoff, the Great Transcription, though everyone—including me—pretended I was there for other, more optimistic, reasons. Further robotic cockroaches turned up, hundreds of them, thousands, often near corpses, sometimes in the prison cells of child-killers being shaved for execution by electric chair, or in the bowel-remains of dying prostitutes gutted by their pimps in Hoboken alleys. Sometimes in AIDS hospices, psychiatric institutions, sensitive areas on overseas military bases, Blockbuster outlets, Disneyland and the myriad food stalls in the Mall of America. They spread through the country like flames over spilled jet fuel...Chicago... Omaha...Portland...Austin...San Diego...you name it. We did what we could to keep the news out of the public arteries. We were lucky, mostly. Then we heard from our contacts in the crumbling Soviet Union, a bloated communism coming down around their ears, that the U.S. wasn't alone in this discreet interplanetary war.

I scanned CNN for signs of the final embarkation, the Weather Channel for indicators of ultimate change, old movies on that Turner station for scenes added while our cultural backs were turned toward something seemingly more interesting. I didn't see a thing. No rough beast, no poltergeist, no worldwide rapture. The earth didn't stop revolving. The final deluge didn't arrive. Everything simply...continued...the way it had always continued...till, that is, the summer of 1994.

I was up in Portland, doing some business at our West Coast headquarters. It'd been a long day, and I was lying on my bed in my hotel room late at night surfing channels when I saw him flip onto the screen. Allegedly killed his ex-wife and her male friend by stabbing them over and over again, then kneeing her spine, yanking back her head by

the blond hair, and slitting her throat. Blood was everywhere. I remember how it was so black it looked as if someone had spattered and puddled crude oil down the condo
walk. And I remember him, the one we soon started calling Rhabhog, standing in the LA police station, proud, de-
termined, even defiant, like this was some inconsequential
project, an ethical fender-bender, like our universe was
somehow smaller than his. I looked into his eyes as his eyes
looked into the media. They said: *You're living on my planet
now.* And a moment later I found myself reaching for the
phone, punching in the numbers, making reservations for
the first flight south in the morning.

You could tell, if you knew the context, if you followed the information. It wasn't hard. The legal wrangling
began, the accusations and counter accusations, the pre-
liminaries, the posturing, the televisual detonation…and I
sat in front of my set in another hotel room in another city
and studied his eyes, the way they'd drift up and left in the
courtroom like his mind was just too busy with important
matters to be troubled by this. The jury selection com-
menced, and the trial itself, and the Dream Team swooped
down, and the experts and counter-experts zigzagged
around the truth, and the DNA discussions erupted, and
the character witnesses came forth, and the videos showing Rhabhog laughing the day his ex-wife died cycled, and
those showing his lame legs, and those showing his legs
weren't lame at all, and the Nazi cop taking repeated de-
tours from the legal boulevard, and the smirk on Rhabhog's
face as he fumbled with that silly bloody glove before the
jury, and the look on his ex-wife's bruised face as she returned from the dead to tell us all he'd get away with it
someday, do what you wanted, think what you would, he'd
get away with it…and I sat in front of my set and studied
his eyes…the way they'd glance up at the camera, checking, the way they'd flirt with the powerful twelve across
the room on his right, sweet as the eyes of a seraphim, the
way they'd roll with disdain when the black man behind

the prosecution's podium made another angry point...the dark brown eyes, flaring, charming, self-pitying, self-righteous, self-aware—and always, if you inspected them close enough, glassy, too...detached...cool...always something calculating as a computer running algorithms behind them.

It wasn't difficult, but we had to be sure. So we brought in the specialists just in case, the kind who don't show up in your phonebook, the kind you'll never find unless they decide to find you, and they went through the footage, played it, replayed it, paused it, zeroed in on that horse-jawed face, that high forehead, that Doberman's neck and chunky shoulders, magnified those eyes with their computers, magnified them some more, till their screens were overrun with them, till there was no more space left for anything else. They went ultra-violet. They went ultrasonic. They went infrared. And then those specialists spotted what we always knew they would: the telltale dark polymer shells, the robotic vidcams pivoting frenetically beneath the surface.

I don't have much time. They're on the landing. The door'll hold them a minute, I figure, maybe a little longer. The Yeltsin-70 will hold them a couple seconds more. There's a gray BMW in the alley out back. I can see it from my window. The phoneline's gone. My cellular's down. This is what it's all about, in the end. This is the thing it all comes down to.

The universe clarified. Everything connected. Everything made perfect sense when it was too late whether it made sense or not. The trial, of course, wormed on. The defense launched its case. The infamous race card pitched into view. The national polls bucked back and forth like a fighter jet tagged by a heat-seeking missile. The police prepared for riots while the talkshows prepared for unimaginable success. My unit moved into the safe house in East LA and prepared to act, readying to pass our amassed data on to other shadowy bureaus with profiles even more nebulous, more intricate and unnameable, than ours. I worked nineteen- and twenty-hour days, slept less and less, but with the dreamless intensity of drugged blackouts…an incorporeal, profound, overweight sleep, the sort where you wake up in exactly the same position in which you lay down, all your digits fizzing with nerve-static.

It was from one of these, on a warm yellow October dawn, that I was roused by a clicking noise like fingernails on a metal desk. White light was everywhere at once. It broke into millions of itself. The cockroach on the pillow next to my ear spoke through the speaker in its belly. Its antennae fidgeted.

"We won," it told me, "the instant the first of us activated its hard-drive."

Its voice was slo-mo, robotic sizzle, white noise.

"There's still the trial, the judge, the jury," I said, groggy.

"It's not about that anymore. It was never about that. Everything's primetime now. Everything's within budget. We know what you know. We've been where you've been."

"You know what you want you to know."

"The judge?"

"He's a fair man. We've checked him out. We can count on him."

"Adopted for an afternoon. Age eight. Picnic in the hills." Clicking. "He doesn't recall. His parents, if asked, remember a different day."

"You contaminated the lines."

"We made him family. His brainstem is our brainstem. His heart, our heart."

I slipped my left hand out from under the thin sheet, lowered it toward the carpeted floor, toward my Yeltsin-70. Light swarmed the room like a photon ocean. I could barely see. Neon red filaments fired up and down my optic thread.

"The jury, then," I said.

"The world is a statistical difficulty, not an impossibility. We knew them before they knew themselves. We…visited."

"The tissue samples ..."

"Cellular reformulation. Nanobots injected into the eye during routine optometric exams. Ascended along the inferior rectus into the braincore. A slow process of reconfiguration. Growth. A flowering."

"They don't act convincingly human..."

"Because they're not convincingly human. Everyone's a talkshow host waiting to happen. Everyone's a book deal in the making. Think beta test. Tv pilot."

"Our planet's your entertainment channel."

"Ten years. Five, all things being equal." I touched cool ceramic. Fingered the safety catch. *Clack.* "Imagine. A galactic atrocity theme park. You should be happy. You should be content. Now you have a purpose. You're becoming a vacation destination." I palmed the oily handle. Trigger. "There are so many sights to see, so many journeys to take."

"We're becoming a moving wax museum."

"You're becoming yourselves. Serial killers. Political assassins. Human sacrifices among the ancient ruins. A full family getaway. And nothing out of the ordinary. All you have to do is be who you are. Cooperate. Help the inevitable process toward the inevitable product. Help happen what will happen without us. Keep your thoughts to yourself."

"Yeah, well, here's the thing."

I rolled off the bed and simultaneously brought up my semi-automatic. The light swamping the room turned pulsating blue. My pillow turned into a haze of smoking feathers. The cockroach turned into steam and shreds.

Only not before it'd broadcast the emergency signal. A high, short, piercing shrill. Not before the end had been set in motion.

A long heart-pump of silence and, milliseconds later, the crash at the front door. Footsteps clumping through the foyer. Rumble on the stairs. My pale hand flying around the bedstand drawer, searching for my cassette.

Beginning the final dispatch, which maybe someone is listening to right now, and which maybe someone isn't...

The apocalypse isn't about clouds of boiling seawater sucked miles into burning atmosphere off the blue coasts of the Bikini atoll. It isn't about the Berlin Wall or the Cuban Blockade or the Butcher of Baghdad, melting polar ice caps or greenhouse gasses or misfiring DNA. It's all about watching. It's all about observing the almost unobservable like a stunned carcrash victim while wondering if what you just saw is real, brakes and flames and palms across the inside of the fiery windshield.

And it is. Every word of it.

It is.

Strategies
in the Overexposure
of Well-Lit Space

37. THE DISCOVERY: CHANNEL
 Kerwin Penumbro, who's taking his birthday off from
his job designing and manufacturing certain popular body
organs (a greasy heart still breathing in a madman's fist is
a perennial favorite, though you should never
underestimate the power of a bluish-white intestines
wrapped on a surprised housewife's fire poker) at the small
Japanese-owned special effects house, Goo & Pwin-Ti, just
off Pioneer Square in Seattle, is expecting maybe a beige
sweater with maroon stripes, or one of those Timex watches
that lets you know the hour in Australia and Greenland
simultaneously and is water-resistant down to a hundred
meters, from his live-in girlfriend, Syndi Shogunn, who Ker
met four years ago in front of the remainders bin at that
just-slightly-kinked record store a block over, The Vinyl
Fetish (Ker looking for the esoteric compilation on Air
Pyrate Muzzik containing every pertinent Beatles song
played backwards, Re:Volver; while Syndi, a secretary over
at the local police station, ferreted for a disc housing themes
to all those really great action-adventures-with-even-a-

vague-connection-to-law-enforcement on the tube from the late sixties and early seventies, to enhance her workplace ambiance, those golden years that brought you "I Spy," "Mannix," "Mission Impossible," "The Man From U.N.C.L.E.," "The F.B.I.," "Batman," "The Fugitive"...a-and even those truly warped masterpieces like "The Prisoner," if you stretched your operational definitions a little...Syndi able to just go on and on about such things), but no way the knock on their apartment door this Thursday morning, Syndi away at the office, coffee spiking the air...not the May sun in Ker's rattled eyes...and certainly not the two men in khaki shirts and khaki pants and five-o'clock stubble at maybe nine-o'clock in the a.m. standing next to the neat cardboard box nearly five feet tall and four feet wide, saying: "Mr. Penumbro? We got your tv here..."

21. IMMORTALITY: STEALTH

A-and not your standard tv, either. Uh-uh. *This* baby is *humongous* and looks like it's been designed in a wind tunnel. It's made out of smooth black plastic and has lots of curves everywhere and Kerwin could under the right circumstances imagine it flying.

Plus it's one of the first HDTV models, the renowned Mitsubishi Stealth.

Plus it comes with one of those incredible mini-satellite deals you hook up outside your window and get like a bazillion channels on.

Kerwin Penumbro falls in love with Syndi Shogunn all over again.

While he's doing so, the delivery people search for the optimum viewing area, 7.4 feet to 13.6 feet from the screen, hook up the cable, adjust the tuning mode to AUTO position, flick the STEREO/MONO switch to STEREO, toy with the convergence panel, the quick-view, the remote.

Instead of breakfast, Ker sits in his bean-bag chair in the middle of the living room like a king on his bamboo throne on a South Pacific island (he's wearing only his grayish jockey shorts, which he knows as well as anyone should really undergo a good washing about now, but, hey…) and studies his owner's manual.

Instead of the nap he planned on taking sometime before noon, he makes himself this monstrous bologna birthday sandwich with lettuce, tomatoes, pickles, a wedge of onion, mustard, and this serious dollop of mayo (the expiration date on the jar barely noticeably out of fashion) on top of which he sprinkles cashews and what's left of his jelly-bean stash, tears open a bag of O'Boise potato chips, and flips the top of a Bud, collapses in his threadbare bean-bag chair 8.3 feet from the black monolith, squirms toward comfort, and clicks the ON button the femtosecond the delivery people nod, shrug, and close the door behind them.

Clicks the OFF button.

Stands, trots into the bedroom, rifles through his sock drawer, finds his last Baby Ruth, shnorks it for an improved disposition on the way back to the living room, squirms into his bean-bag chair like John Glenn into Friendship 7, clicks the ON button.

Clicks the OFF button.

Stands, trots into the bathroom, thumbs down the front of his Fruit of the Looms, relaxes his urethra, stares at the high-gloss ceiling (across which scrolls a single ant) while listening with pride to the vigorous plashing below, wriggles himself dry, pops the front of his Fruit of the Looms into place, whistling without really realizing he's whistling (the reverse version of "Strawberry Fields," doncha know), feels the sugar from the Baby Ruth beginning to itch the glassy horizon of his brain, trots back to the living room, squirms into his bean-bag chair, chomps into his sandwich, clicks the ON button.

Clicks the OFF button.

Stands, trots into the bedroom, throws on a pair of jeans and sneakers and a Sick Poppies t-shirt (this black woodcut of a sleeping head, python-long tongue lolling out and curling below like a garden hose, on a white background), trots into the kitchen, searches the top drawer beside the stove for his keys, grabs his black denim jacket in whose pocket he knows resides every penny he possesses for the remainder of the month (more than two weeks to go…a-and how did *that* happen?), jogs onto the porch, down the external wooden staircase, down the block to the 7-Eleven where he purchases a pint of Cherry Garcia, his fave, from an underfed chestnut-colored man without a thumb on his left hand…

Jogs up the block, up the external wooden staircase, onto the porch, into the kitchen, down the hall, back to the kitchen where he picks up a spoon and deposits said keys and jacket, down the hall again, into the living room, into the bean-bag chair, and, panting, clicks the ON button once more…

5. PRIME: TIME: LIVE
Kerwin Penumbro experiences his consciousness expand in a flood of sucrose-enhanced light.

141. DUCK & COVER
Nona Nova, hospital nurse, has battled illness on the eleven-to-seven shift. She has shocked a cardiac victim back from the brink of death; uncovered a plot by fiendish candy-striper Stephanie Stix to kill elderly patients; eased Dale Devin, young doctor, from his depression brought on by his wife Dolly's abscondence, a pending malpractice suit, and by his youngest son, little Donny Devin, dying in a freak fiery plane crash in the Andes (fog; tribal blow-gun competition); cheered up a child laced with tumors; unraveled the labyrinthian financial problems gnawing at Dustin Elwood, hospital head. Nona is thus understandably tired now. Her legs feel like hardening cement. Her head feels like twelve feet under a swimming pool. Her body feels old at twenty-seven. She stands in the restroom, staring forlornly in the mirror at the mulberry sleep-bruises gathered below her methylene-blue eyes, unzips her

uniform, reveals her tight belly, almond-brown skin, pert breasts barely hidden under bra. She runs warm water in the sink. Splashes her face. Reaches for a handful of paper towels. When she looks in the mirror again another head floats behind hers: Rex Rory, flamboyant resident.

Nona Nova ducks and covers.

246. CARTOON GEL: HOMELESSNESS: LIGHT

Kerwin Penumbro claps in unabashed delight, forgetting he's holding the bologna sandwich, which pretty much disintegrates in his lap. Unfazed, he reconstructs it as best he can and takes another bite and smacks in nirvanic satisfaction.

Because it's like living in a cartoon gel; the colors are so bright; the outlines so crisp.

Everything is animation rich.

A-and the sound…the sound is…Ker believes he feels spittle collecting along his busy lower lip.

Which totally undercuts the theory he developed as a philosophy major for his undergraduate honors thesis back at U.W., which states that imagination and desire continually outstrip technology…as in we're always waiting for the transistors to catch up with the synapses, always able to out-think the next mechanical or digital advance.

Nope.

He was wrong.

This appliance just about does it.

Though, true, nonetheless, that, weh-hell…look at computers.

If your basic car advanced at the same rate your basic computer did over the past two decades or whatnot, you'd be looking at a vehicle that'd travel at like five-hundred-thousand miles an hour, get a million miles to the gallon, and cost less than a down payment on a Stealth like this.

Which is simply to say things have gotten pretty…what.

Weird.

For instance, look at Ker looking at himself looking at the box, Ker thinks, looking. You'd imagine he was watching a really interesting sex arrangement through a one-way mirror when in fact he is watching this maybe awful soap opera which he simply can't turn away from.

Culture's first perceptual orifice, his theory goes, which is in fact someone else's theory, he's pretty sure, but, hey, was your no-frills cave door: primary purpose of allowing hominidal passage.

Culture's second, once we'd gotten beyond those load-bearing external walls, was, natch, the window: primary purpose of facilitating movement of light and air.

And but culture's third window?

Well, you're looking at it.

Or looking at Ker looking at himself look at it.

Except you don't look *out* through the third window, do you, reasons Ker. Can't. You look *in*. But the In you're looking at pretends it's an Out, which it sometimes is, sort of, if you think about it. Plus it's not so much that *you* look in or out as *it* looks in or out, kind of borrowing your eyes from you and every now and then forgetting to give them back. Plus what it does, honestly, is to bring stuff outside inside, such as it is, though the outside stuff pretends to be outside stuff when it's in fact inside stuff, as in produced and edited and so forth, and though it makes you feel you're always somewhere else when you're in truth always doing nothing much more than, like Ker here, feeling the spittle form on your lower lip while participating in the rampant overexposure of well-lit space, taking another bite of that really fabulous sandwich in a world without borders, because, if you stop and think about it, your home becomes someone else's home, doesn't it, your digital front door always being open, and not exactly yours, even while it's yours...

Which is to say nothing of stuff like e-mail a-and telephones a-and radios a-and...

Ker interrupts himself to wonder if he's heard, or only imagined he's heard, that there exists a model of the Mitsubishi Stealth that comes with a catheter for a prolonged viewing experience.

He'll have to order the catalog and check it out.

18. ROSES: TEACUP: REVOLVER

"You no good varmint!" the barrel-chested man in the white cowboy hat at the breakfast table is saying. Ker blinks. A tidy breakfast table. Three roses in a crystal vase. White tablecloth. Beflowered china. Tinkle of teacups. "You polecat!" he says. "You think you can plan my daddy's downfall and get away with it? You think you can sabotage his oil wells and mama and me'd sit still for it? Lickin' my boots is too good for you."

The barrel-chested man in the black cowboy hat smirks.

"An' what you gonna do about it?" he asks.

"This!" the barrel-chested man in the white cowboy hat shouts, flipping an oily blue revolver into view.

211. AS SEEN ON TV

A-and faxes a-and beepers a-and cell phones a-and the World Wide Web a-and voice mail a-and answering machines a-and (in a sense, at any rate) VCRs a-and stereos a-and videocams a-and...

98. HE LEARNS HOW TO LOSE GRACEFULLY

Rope-and-log bridge wobbling over ravine.

Skydiver in red, white and blue jumpsuit. Lightning bolts on his helmet. Parachute on his back. Flawless teeth in his grin. He raises two fingers to his forehead in a flip salute to posterity, gingerly climbs over the cable, poises, arches his back, leaps toward the river threading below.

He plummets like a starfish.

You wait one one-thousand, two one-thousand, three.

He plummets like a car heading through the railing in an action adventure.

There is no white bouquet of chute, no slowing of momentum, no noise save the whipping of wind far above the tiny red, white, and blue dot.

You watch him begin to flap his arms, a little at first, then harder and harder.

77. UNCLE BUDDY'S PHANTOM FUNHOUSE

Teenagers believe they are immortal, says this Rod-Serlingesque voice as the camera pans through the wooded night, which is clearly a Hollywood day seen through a special filter, fake car lights wobbling through fake pines on a lonely fake gravel road. *They believe nothing will ever happen to them. They live on their own psychic planet in a world where deodorant, hair style, jeans length, acoustic preference and mouthwash products matter deeply. They sleep profoundly, steadily, having all the dreams they should have...except these five teenagers on their way to this desolate farmhouse somewhere in upstate New York, who are under the false impression they are moving through a sexual and psychic rite of passage called a Wild Weekend at Uncle Buddy's Hunting Cabin that will involve alcohol, tobacco, and firearms, not to mention certain acts of unprotected mildly illegal bodily combinations, will die tonight, and die horribly, one by one, mostly in nothing but their underwear, their breaths a hive of plaque and pre-gingivital fear at the hands of*

183. RUBBER WIG: CHILDBIRTH: HOMICIDE

"I's a killer," announces weeping Bobbie Joe Sue Alice Mary Bobson, who according to the ID at the bottom of the screen is a seamstress living in a trailer park in northwestern Florida.

Her hair reminds Kerwin of whipped cream in its hue and shape.

She will be buried in a piano case, it occurs to him, she's so fat.

"Share your pain with us," urges psychic healer Abbey Rode, whose hair reminds Kerwin of a red rubber wig. Abbey has that slack-muscled serious-yet-utterly-accepting face that only drugged children and talk-show psychic healers have. "We're here for you."

Abbey reaches out and pats Bobbie Joe Sue Alice Mary on the wrist.

Bobbie Joe Sue Alice Mary snorfles.

"My stepfather and his minister done abused my second cousin Pattie Bob Anne Frankie Patson when she was eleven."

"Sexually?"

"Snorfle snorfle."

Pan to empathetic audience faces riveted by the drama unfolding before them.

"What happened?"

"Done got her with child."

"Pregnant?"

"Snorfle."

"What happened next?"

"I didn't know none of this till last year, see. Only one night I's sittin' in my hot tub out back with my boyfriend Billy Ray Tom John, and Billy Ray Tom John? He turns to me and says somethin' real rude about my weight and all displacing the water and pretty much emptyin' the tub out, so I's feel liken to kill him. And then it all comes afloodin' back."

"The water?"

"The memories. All this red and purple. Scares me something awful. So I's of course calls the Psychic Healer Hotline."

"And one of my Hot Helpers talks to you..."

"Betty Earla Clarissa Lisa Simpson. Yep. And they knows somethin's real wrong right away, havin' second sight and all, so they's pass me on to you."

"Dhambala be thanked."

"Snorfle snorfle snorfle."

"…?"

"And then you and me, we come to meet and all and you redresses me to my former life and all, only afore we get there I take this what you call it detour and sees me afloatin' in my momma's womb…only I ain't alone."

"You're not?"

"I got me a brother I ain't never heard about. I's never had no brother before, see? I can tell he's my twin. He's in there with me. And then I start rememberin'."

"…?"

"He done raped me in my momma's womb. Every day. I'd just be, like, hangin' there and he'd come up and whump me and have his way with me and all. I's become my twin-brother fetus's sex slave. It's…snorfle snorfle…herbal."

"Herbal?"

"Turbal."

"Terrible. Yes. What did you do next?"

"I's takes it at fust. What's a baby-girl fetus gonna do? Only then, as my brain and amatomy develops some more and all, I's starts aplannin'. Float and watch. Float and watch. And I's wait till he's asleepin', see?"

"…?"

"It's night time, I knows, cuz I can hear my cousin-momma outside snorin' like a chainsaw gnashin' on a metal flag pole, and I real careful like just reach over and slip his umbilical cord round his neck, see? Never forgets the way his eyes sorta pop open, neither, all filled with surprise and hurt and all, and how he just starts aflippin' and aflappin' 'round in there like a hotcake on a griddle. Only thing is? Thing is, more he struggles, faster he dies."

"You murdered your own brother?"

Pan to shocked audience faces.

"We was born premature, him and me, only I done survived. My momma never told me about him, except I knowed. I'm a survivor. Been survivin' fer near a ten hunert years."

"Ten hundred..."

"That's who I is. Ever since I's fought the choppy Atlantic waters so me and my kin could discover Vinland."

"Vinland?"

"Vinland."

"As in..."

"That was me in my purvious life."

"The New World?"

"1000 A.D., give er take a month or two. Yup. Ol' Chris Columbus couldn't find a possum in his own britches..."

222. PLAY: SIN

Not long ago our culture believed play was a waste of time, an avuncular announcer's voice says, *a distraction from the truly important matters that kept a society whole and functioning. Some even regarded it as a punishable sin, the devil's work that chipped away at serious moral pursuits. But now most psychologists believe play is a necessary part of growing up. It helps children develop healthy attitudes and bodies. It paradoxically instills a sense of following rules and allows a chance for children to vent their excess energy. Recreational activities teach children to get along with others. The personality of a child grows as he or she learns new skills and develops confidence in sports—motor, sensory, or intellectual. In competitive games, he or she learns how to lose gracefully.*

59. THE GREAT WHEEL SPINS

The great wheel spins. The audience shouts. The game show host smiles confidently. Mabel Utta, sixty-two, from Dayton, Ohio, with a son in the Navy, jumps up and down, her fat chugging, and claps her tiny hands in glee.

1001. PRIME: TIME: LIVE

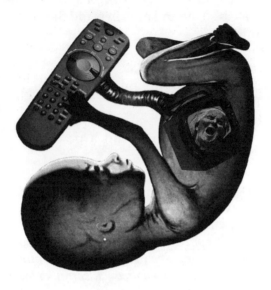

6. ART: CRIMES

Yeah, well, um…this is it? We startin'?… What? Oh. My name is…my working name is Zondi. No. Just Zondi. No. Fuck the parental-naming thing. That's all about social control and shit. I was raised in Hackensack, New Jersey. I live on the Lower East Side now. Yeah. I'm a performance artist…. What? Yeah. I knew it was my calling for like friggin' forever. When I was thirteen or something I saw this thing in this underground zine about this woman who performed surgery on herself and televised the operations around the world. I forget her name. She's dead now, I think. Liver transplant. Only I knew then I had what it took to be a performance artist…. What? Oh, so no, the fucking bourgeois art establishment wouldn't accept me. That's the thing. That's how it all started. Fucking tight-assed fuckheads. I couldn't get in to even like a single art school. They said I didn't have no talent cuz I couldn't draw or paint or nothing. So I said fuck that. Those guys' conscienceness is like the size of a gnat's butt. I majored in communications. Which is what took me to Fairleigh Dickinson, right, which is this nest of cheesy reactionary fascists. They flunked me in math and social sciences and composition and a couple of other things I forget. So I said fuck that. I'd make it on my own. Which is what took me to the city, where I met Mongo…. What? Right. Just Mongo. He's a good guy. He thinks and everything. He once studied with what's-his-face. And so he introduced me to the idea of AIDS…Arts In Denial & Shit…which it deals with art that denies it's art and all, you know, as in graphic design, only that gave me the idea for my magum okus…. What? I'm nineteen…. What? One-point-two million. Yeah. So anyways, I go to myself: fuck the commodrification of the arts on the fins of the millemmium. Fuck the fascist market. Fuck art dealers who wipe their asses with the masters like, you know, everybody. And, blam, right there in this nice café on the Lower East Side this cool post-strucuralistic concept of my magum okus hits me: NOT. Get it?… What? Right. So I decide I won't create a fucking thing for the rest of my life. See? *That's* my project. It's an act of negation deal, like. No paintings, no sculptures, no lithographs, no videos, no mobiles, no prints, no assemblages, no collages, no sketches, no nothing. See? I might do it with a punk rock band too. It's a statement…. What? I don't know. What you think it means?… What? Sleep late, I guess. Listen to music. Last year I took up sailing…right after I joined that yacht club thing over on Long Island…which is pretty cool. I really like tv. Cartoons, mostly. "N.Y.P.D. Blue" has a very naturalistic perspective on our fascist society today which is pretty cool…. What? Sure I got a VCR. Who doesn't?… What? Yeah, I guess. It's okay. I don't miss it. I don't miss it at all. Lately I've been thinking about taking up teaching. I figure maybe it's time to give something back…

13. SHE LEARNS HOW TO LOSE GRACEFULLY
      She's already tired. Her legs feel like hardening cement. Her body feels old at nineteen. She stands in the back

bedroom on the first floor of Uncle Buddy's Hunting Cabin and stares forlornly at herself in the mirror. Tom isn't the gentleman she had imagined. Or maybe Tim is the gentleman she had imagined. It's hard to tell. She unzips her jeans, skins them off, shrugs her Sick Poppies t-shirt over her head. She runs warm water in the shower. Her breasts beneath her lace bra. Reaches for the Ivory soap on the sink ledge. Her name is Melinda. Or maybe it's Glenda. Or Brenda. Ker either wasn't paying attention when it was mentioned or it wasn't mentioned in the first place. When Melinda or Glenda or Brenda looks in the steamy mirror again another head floats behind hers.

Zodiac Killer, homicidal maniac. Bright brown eyes. Flawless teeth in the mouth hole of his ski-mask.

He raises two fingers to his forehead in a flip salute to posterity.

The first teenager, wearing lace panties and bra, ducks and covers.

An ice pick glints in the shadows above her fourteen gallons of bleached-blond hair.

She opens her mouth to scream.

The ice pick descends.

The first teenager senses mortality.

201. THE DISCOVERY: CHANNEL

"Uh, hey…" Ker says, beer can pausing maybe two centimeters from his lips.

He leans forward.

Wasn't that…yeah…hey…wasn't that *Syndi's* face in the audience-reaction shot back there?

Okay, so maybe it took a couple of minutes to register, but fer shure it was, has to be…just after that what's-her-name, fat lady with the whipped-cream hair, admitted she whacked her own fraternal twin in flagrante utero.

Steady, boyo. Steady.

He leans back.

Lessee.

Okay, Take Two: there was this anorexic mom-type with green turtle-shell glasses next to a black rodential woman with simpatico tears in her eyes...a-and right behind them, bobbing just out of focus, was... Syndi...yeah, Syndi...Ker'd of course recognize her anywhere...long honey hair in a ponytail...wire-rimmed glasses...slightly puzzled brown eyes...almost like Ker wasn't the only one wondering why she was there...

Only...why *was* she there?

She's supposed to be at work today, right? Plus she's never mentioned the Psychic Healer Network. Plus that show was shot...where? New York, probably, or Chicago.

Creeeeeepy.

Ker shudders.

Weh-hell...these things were always prerecorded, weren't they, bordering as they always did on a species of well-disguised infomercials, and, uh, Ker guesses it was just possible this was taped like four years and one day ago, twenty-four hours before he stepped into The Vinyl Fetish, or maybe seventy-two, or maybe three months, which isn't the point, is it, but nonetheless...maybe it represents just one of those little secrets lovers keep from one another, or...not so much secrets (Ker simply couldn't contemplate such a thing hanging between Syndi and him like one of his body organs on the drying hooks down at work)...as just, um, what...just unexplored psychological territory that would under the right circumstances become totally mapped.

Unless, it goes without saying...unless it *wasn't* Syndi, but one of those look-alikes you see all the time on the streets around town who you could *swear* was like Ellen DeGeneres or that woman from "Friends" or something, except wasn't.

Right?

With one hand Ker tips back the Bud for a long mind-clearing swig and with the other flips channels in reverse, descending the decision tree, trying to relocate that show...only the thing is...the thing is...he can't.

Okey-dokey. Not to worry, he thinks, starting, needless to say, to worry. Not to panic. He's been hopping around a lot, and hasn't a clue where exactly he's been.

It's all right.

No sweat.

A-and he hasn't been looking at the time...so for all he knows the show is already off the air, replaced by an infomercial about how to hit it rich by buying all these houses in Arizona or investing in Rogaine or something, o-or maybe another guest and host are on in the second segment (if indeed the fat woman and healer comprised the first), o-or maybe there's a commercial cycling and so he's in fact looking at the right channel but it feels like he's looking at the wrong one.

"Shit," Ker announces, clicking.

This horrendous green snot bubble balloons out some pig-snouted female kid's left nostril and the well-dressed woman across from her at the nice LA restaurant begins spontaneously kecking.

Click.

A woman with stelliform shoe-polish black hair's head derricks up and down in a man's naked lap.

Click.

Prosthetic surgery is painful, but it can powerfully renew our sense of involvement in the world. It's all a question of where you locate the information interface: how much you can stand to lop off, or just how far back you're willing to go...

Click.

A reddish-brown male *Cimex lectularius* (bedbug to you and me) in ghastly close-up stabs its beak into a female's abdomen, preparing to release its sperm into her wound and hence bloodstream.

Click.

Tribal drums and primitive wails blossom. Colors whirl. Black men in grass skirts and jangling brass earrings, bracelets, and necklaces dance wildly around a bonfire, shaking spears, lifting knees, hooting and jabbering at the nightspirits. Their earlobes hang to their jawbones. Scars funnel their cheeks. Only the whites of their eyes show. Ker believes they're real, but feels there's an equal chance he's just watching a rerun of "Gilligan's Island." They leap and caper around a naked pale body tied to the ground, ready for sacrifice. Arms stretched out to the sides. Legs wide apart. The face alert, familiar…very familiar…

Click.

A-and it's…it's…OUTTA HERE!!!

111. AS SEEN ON TV

44. DUCK & COVER

"What you gonna do about it?" the barrel-chested man in the black cowboy hat asks.

Ker feels in familiar territory and settles back in his bean-bag chair.

"This!" the barrel-chested man in the white cowboy hat shouts, flipping an oily blue revolver into view.

"Good lord God, *no!*" the mother in the white cowboy hat cries, trying to stand, crinkled and old.

The barrel-chested man in the black cowboy hat tries to duck and cover. But it's too late. The barrel-chested man in the white cowboy hat fires. China crashes. Crystal splinters. A chair cracks against the floor.

"*Uggggh!*" the mother in the white cowboy hat cries, fatally wounded.

111. AS SEEN ON TV
"Say what?" Ker says.

249. AS A SOAP OPERA
It is also worth mentioning that although egg consumption in the United States is one-half of what it was in 1945, there has not been a comparable decline in heart disease. Moreover, although the American Heart Association deems eggs hazardous, a diet without them can be equally hazardous. Not only do eggs have the most perfect protein components of any food, but they al

3.

68. DUCK & COVER

A glistening black Porsche sizzes through what looks like downtown Dallas or downtown Miami late at night, screeching around corners, turboing through intersections. A Corvette jets down avenue after avenue, low slung, white, locked in overdrive. Scattered gunfire. Because of the rapid jump-cuts, it's unclear exactly who's chasing who. Closeup of Rex Rory behind the wheel of one of the cars (though which is unclear), perspiration sparkling on his face, fury in his eyes, hatred at mouth corners...most likely, given the context, not playing the flamboyant resident (though this obviously is open to debate and readjustment through viewing time)...followed by the closeup of that barrel-chested man in the black cowboy hat, sweat sparkling on his face, eyes wide with fear, nose now broken and swelling, who isn't, in fact, Ker is almost sure, the guy from the other show, though it's possible he is, in which case next week's episode is playing simultaneously with this week's, only on a different channel, or maybe the syndicated version of the show (whose name is on the tip of Ker's tongue) from let's say two years ago is cycling simultaneously with the so-far-non-syndicated version, only on a different channel. Ker in any case has the sense that he's missed too many pieces of the plot to understand very much. An excess of lines has been spoken without him there to hear. He might as well give up. Plus he has the feeling he's seen this one before...until, that is, the wedge-shaped spaceship appears, a glowing green delta over the city, and simply tremendous, as in the size of a hovering battleship, and it's busy shooting some sort of photon-torpedo-looking jobs at *both* cars, only the aliens inside are really bad aims and keep nuking wads of unsuspecting tourists who have no right to be standing on street corners at this time of night in this kind of iffy neighborhood anyway. Until, that is, the camera zips inside said ship, and Ker sees the two standard-issue cute human kids at the control panels,

maybe twelve or thirteen years old, all agitated, trying to
fly this thing and clearly pushing the wrong buttons by
accident, and it dawns on Ker this whole business is really
a comedy, the kids having crept aboard said craft probably
built by dad in Utah or something and bumped the throttle
without knowing it and now are on some kind of
cartoonish joyride, ha ha…unless, uh-oh, Ker thinks, they
aren't kids at all, but scary kids-appearing aliens, maybe
pod-kids, and this ducks-in-a-barrel thing is their idea of
a good time, and maybe they aren't on earth at all, but on
their home planet, a-and this is simply their playground
out back or in their cellar, a-and the guys in the cars and
all the bystanders have been unknowingly kidnapped and
transported here while they slept, a-and still believe
they're in Dallas or Miami, which from their perspective
is being invaded, which is a possibility definitely worth
considering, in which case it's really a horror film that's
super-intelligently conceived, though Ker kind of doubts
it, but decides to go along with the flow anyway, since
it'll make his viewing more palatable. Until one of the
kids or pod-kids or whatever lifts a can of something
apparently called a Zerp soft-drink and takes a chug
followed by a wide satisfied smile, and the announcer,
this French guy who sounds like he's on barbiturates, says
something Ker can't understand, though he once back-
packed through France for two weeks, and in college took
two years of the stuff, and Ker realizes he's been inhabiting
a commercial masquerading as a horror film
masquerading as a comedy masquerading as an action
adventure masquerading as a soap opera.

76. NEWS: BREAK
    A blueblack fly alights on the eyebrow of a young
black boy whose facial skin has shrunk and withered like

666. HOPE FLOATS

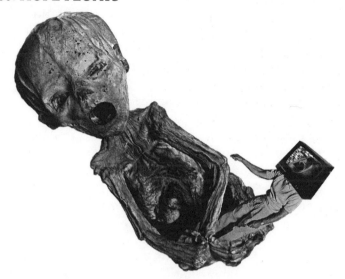

99. THE GREAT WHEEL SPINS

The great wheel spins, brilliant light fizzling like fireworks. The audience shouts insanely. The game show host smiles confidently. Bertha Marcella, fifty-eight, from What Cheer, Iowa, with a son in the Marines, jumps up and down, her fat chugging, and claps her tiny hands in glee.

Then a shadow crosses her face.

She feels the pang.

Feels the elephant sitting on her chest.

The lightning in her left arm.

Her face muscles slacken. Her hands drop to her sides. Her eyes look up at the ceiling in disbelief. Bertha opens her mouth, sticks out her tongue, and topples over backwards.

She is wearing, Ker notices, a Timex on her left wrist.

31. THE DISCOVERY: CHANNEL

A cartoon dustcloud churns across the cartoon desert under a cartoon sky that's eerily pink instead of blue.

LANCE OLSEN

It's Wile E. Coyote. He's wearing a pair of Acme rocket boots. And the Roadrunner is doing that thing the Roadrunner always does, just kind of gliding nonchalantly along on those whirling legs of his...cool, calm, dum-de-dum, with even this like semi-reptilian smirk carved into its beak.

Only something's wrong here.

Ker expects those rocket boots to blow up any second. Or, you know, a huge rock or cactus to zoom out of the desertscape and slam the poor carnivore so hard he can't stop vibrating for the remainder of the episode. O-or maybe some other gadget he tried to use earlier in the skit (an anvil, say, or an Acme ICBM, or a turbo-powered car right out of the Jetsons' garage) to appear and burn his sorry ass to a crisp cinder.

Since, as Ker and every other philosophy major who's ever watched this show knows, Wile E. is none other than the animational embodiment of Sisyphus, and the Roadrunner his boulder, and the desert his hill, and the poor guy is just never going to win; it's so obvious it hurts. He's going to fall, explode, leap faithless into oblivion, squish, become existential flypaper for every bit of bad karma the uncaring universe can dish out. That's the given. But his dignity (oh, yeah, have no doubt about it, folks: that's *dignity* you're witnessing there) arises from the fact that he *knows* this and just keeps on going anyway, fuck the degenerate swine at Acme, you've got to *believe*.

Except...he's gaining ground, is the thing.

Wile E. Coyote's actually closing the gap. There goes another ten yards, and another five, and he's stretching both arms out in front of him, sort of leaning into the momentum as the exact same background cycles over and over again behind him, and the Roadrunner is actually looking over its shoulder, a little nervous now, that frozen smirk beginning to melt, and Wile E. reaches down to the control panel on his belt and hits OVERDRIVE.

Zooooooooooom!

And, *wham*, he's got him!

Yep.

Wile E. grabs the Roadrunner by the neck with one hand and turns off his rocket boots with the other and there they suddenly are, huffing in the silent desert, orange sun beginning to set behind them.

Holy fucking cow.

Only...hey...what's that?

They...*embrace*! Yeah, and if the truth be known there's nothing female about that big bird and...what the hell's *that* all about???

The Roadrunner slips Wile E. his tongue, and Wile E. reciprocates, a-and pretty soon it sort of inches up on Ker that the Roadrunner's just been playing hard to get all this time...yeah, that's it, the whole thing's been one big come-on...and now what you've got yourself here are two really randy cartoon characters, a-and...whoah...old Wile E.'s getting down on his paws and knees...a-and the Roadrunner's kind of shuffling up behind him...a-and, *arggggh*, that ain't no tongue, man, that ain't no beak...

169. THE LOVEBOAT

Nona Nova, hospital nurse, stares forlornly at herself in the mirror, unzips her uniform, reveals her tight belly, bronze skin, pert breasts barely hidden under lacy bra. She runs warm water in the sink. Splashes her face. Reaches for a handful of paper towels. When she looks in the mirror again another head floats behind hers: Rex Rory, flamboyant resident. Nona cracks a smile.

Rex steps into the women's restroom quickly and shuts the door behind him, flashes her a flawless grin.

They embrace.

"Oh god, how I've missed you!" Nona murmurs into his ear.

He squeezes.

"Yes, yes, yes!" he whispers.

They kiss.

She reaches for his belt. He reaches for her breasts. For her belly. For the astonishing curve of her spine.

"Hey, wait a second," he says, feeling that weird bulge in her panties. "What's this?"

33. DUCK & COVER

51. A PRICK

The male platypus possesses a hollow claw, or spur, on each hind leg. The spurs are connected with poison glands. The platypus pricks and poisons its enemies when it feels threatened.

9. PRIME: TIME: LIVE

There is no white bouquet of chute, no slowing of momentum, no sound save the whipping of wind far above the tiny red, white, and blue dot.

You watch him flap his arms.

Watch him kick his legs.

Speed down, faster and faster. Shoot down. Hum down. Hurtle straight for the jagged rocks and shallow river below. The strong current. The icy water.

The twisted bodies of those who tried and failed before him.

188. ADDRESS AT VISION 31

"Uh-oh," Kerwin says, glancing at the last bite of his sandwich pinched between his thumb and forefinger.

He isn't feeling so hot all of a sudden.

His stomach's queasy and his head's all...it's kind of like when you have the flu and the rest of the world looks like you're squinting through a layer of Saran Wrap someone's coiled around you.

He starts giving some serious thought to that mayonnaise.

It *did* taste sort of funny.

Sour, like.

He puts the last bite of his sandwich on the end-table next to his bean-bag chair and, weh-hell, just leaves it.

Plus he hasn't been paying attention to the time, but now the light in the room's changed for the unmistakably more somber, taken on a resolutely late-afternoon hue, unless obviously the sky has clouded up, in which case it could be any time of the day...only he senses Syndi should be here by now. The apartment should be full of her presence. He should be smelling dinner cooking. He should be listening to her tell him about her day as she tinkers in the kitchen.

Maybe it *wasn't* her on that show...

After all, the idea didn't even suggest itself until minutes later, did it, which only goes to prove how the mind isn't always what it's cracked up to be, you know?

Maybe Syndi has a twin sister...did he ever think of that?

O-or maybe not a twin so much as a sister who looks enough like her to be mistaken for her twin sister.

Only Syndi doesn't know because they were separated at birth.

O-or maybe it's possible, given the ultimately limited genetic resources on the planet, that someone shares enough of her cellular patterns that on a tv, across great distances, she could easily pass as Syndi.

It could happen, Kerwin thinks, reaching for his beer and then deciding against it.

Fer shure.

Why not?

3. OPEN HEART MESSAGE

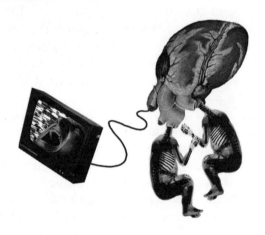

107. VINYL FETISH

Mildred Openheimer, sixty-three, from Onaway, Idaho, with a son in the Air Force, opens her mouth, sticks out her tongue, and topples over backwards. She hits the floor like a whale dropped from a 747.

Just at the moment the wheel stops spinning.

Just at the second its arrow points to JACKPOT.

Just at the instant sirens begin to shriek and buzzers to trill and alarms to rattle.

The game show host, Sam Slant, close-cropped graying beard and slicked-back hair, still smiling, looks down at Mildred, up at the camera, over at the other contestants.

"Um," he says.

Which leads Ker to assume he's watching a speedily goofed-up game show until the two detectives in black, one short and one tall, one chubby and one underfed, walk out on stage and it becomes clear this is the old game-show-within-a-police-show trope.

At which time Ker realizes Mildred is being played by Sandi Slam, the same young actress who plays Nona Nova, only she's all decked out in layers of foam to make her look huge and old, which impresses Ker a lot, from a professional point of view.

But not as much as the explanation that the short chubby detective with a head shaped vaguely like a hammer delivers, hardly moving his lips, as paramedics begin to work on poor Mildred whose mouth is opening and closing like a pithed frog's.

Mildred Openheimer, unhappily married to one Marvin Openheimer, and unhappily mothered to Murray, Mini, and Mimmi Openheimer, and feeling really alone way out there in Onaway, Idaho, became involved with the Internet as a way to meet people. She joined a number of chat groups. One of them, which she thought had to do with discussing old-time records, was called The Vinyl Fetish and was frequented by all manner of S&M types, one of whom went by the moniker Slowhand.

Mildred fell through the looking glass, discovering a world with him she never knew existed.

And she liked what she discovered.

So before long she took on the handle Black Widow, having very little appellative imagination left, given all that time in that little town, and off they went.

At first Mildred and Slowhand gabbed nightly in the chat space while Marvin stared at the tube just a couple of feet away, spinning all manner of increasingly sicko fantasies to basically pass the time...except then they gradually elided into e-mail correspondence, where suffice it to say the words *tit clamps, penis rings,* and *nice fucking slow strangulation* came up a whole bunch more frequently than in what you might conceptualize as conventional day-to-day friendly discourse.

One morning a month ago Mildred waited for Marvin and the kids to leave for work and school, respectively, packed a suitcase, and, without even scribbling an adios note, vamoosed, traveling via train to LA where Slowhand (aka one Ralph Schnorz, a five-o'clock-stubble-at-nine-in-the-morning kind of guy if ever there was one) was waiting.

They met at a hotel where Schnorz employed some of the ideas on Mildred they'd been discussing digitally, then went downtown where they got her on this game show, The Great Wheel Spins, and, seconds before she took the stage, fed her three prophylactics packed with heroin, each with a hairline tear in it, which ruptured the eyeblink she began jumping up and down, releasing enough diacetylmorphine into her system to kill something like eighteen elephants and maybe a lion and water buffalo besides, executing the sadomasochistic double-suicide pact they'd been weaving for almost a year, which means...

"Hic, hic, hic," Sam Slant, game-show host, says, beginning to gag. "Hic, hic, hic."

He reaches up and with a flourish yanks off his beard and toupee, revealing, yep, the bald-headed pock-marked five-o'clock-shadowed features of none other than Ralph Schnorz, sadomasochistic killer, who has himself just bitten down on a cyanide capsule he bought on a recent trip to Tijuana, but not before ripping away his clip-on tie, popping the buttons down the front of his white Armani shirt, and dipping inside for one more yank on the biggest tit clamps you've ever seen, more like something you'd find on a worktable in a hobby shop or even steel-smelting factory than anything you'd ever expect to find on your average human body, at which point the *real* Sam Slant lurches up in the middle of the audience, burbling mostly to himself as *his* hit of heroin finishes its work, and topples face forward onto unsuspecting Mabel Utta, sixty-two, from Dayton, Ohio, with a son in the Navy, whose osteoporosed neck snaps instantly, actually detaching from her body in a geyser of blood and tumbling bowling-ball-like through the initially baffled and then increasingly horrified audience, sending blue-haired women right and left into immediate cardiac ricti, not to mention one of the lighting guys wearing khaki shirt and pants, one Billy Ray Tom John, recently arrived from Florida on the heels of a really ugly breakup with his really ugly girlfriend, her adipose tissue still giving him nightmares, who dies quickly and almost painlessly, but not before thumbing the switch that sends several tons of klieg lights hurtling down on the two detectives who duck and cover...but without much lasting success.

431. LOOKING GLASS GEYSER

199. AS A SOAP OPERA

Rex Rory, flamboyant resident, slaps her. Punches her on the shoulders.

Nona Nova, hospital nurse, laughs at his foolish lopsided smacks.

"You no good bitch!" he yells. "You trollop! You whelp! You malfeasor! You think I'm just another one of your toys you can play with and throw away? You think you can sleep with me and turn round and sleep with my sister, my own *sister*, Rita Rory, without a thought? Well, you can't! You're gonna pay for this! You're gonna wished you never laid eyes on me!"

Nona Nova flashes him one of her flawless patented grins.

"And how, pray tell, do you think you're going to accomplish that?" she asks.

"Like *this!*" Rex Rory, flamboyant resident, shouts, flipping an oily blue revolver into view.

113. REVOLVER

"And so," Paul McCartney says, interviewing (if Ker's not mistaken) Marshall McLuhan on some minimalist powder-blue set, "the thing is, aren't we talking about an ideological shift in the social dominant, really?"

"Er, um, right," McLuhan says, running a nervous hand across his salt-and-pepper hair, obviously surprised to find himself talking to this rock legend. "Because, um, well, all media, from the phonetic alphabet to the computer, are extensions of man that cause deep and lasting changes in him and transform his environment. Such an extension is an intensification, an amplification of an organ, sense or function, and whenever it takes place, the central nervous system appears to institute a self-protective *numbing* of the affected area..."

"Insulates and anesthetizes it from conscious awareness, doesn't it?"

"A process rather like that which occurs to the body under shock or stress conditions, or to the mind in line with the Freudian concept of repression."

"So what you're saying, really, is that multiple subjectivities can't articulate their circumscribed 'reality'— to employ a perhaps-outdated social construct—can they, until they've moved beyond that positional matrix?"

McLuhan shoots McCartney a half-lidded suspicious glance.

"The...um...right...Most people cling to what I call the rearview-mirror view of their world. By this I mean to say that because of the invisibility of any environment during the period of its innovation, man is only consciously aware of the environment that has *preceded* it. In other words, an environment becomes fully visible only when it has been superseded by a new environment. Thus we're always one step behind in our view of the world."

"So what you're suggesting is that the ideological imperative becomes recontextualized only through a spacio-temporal reconfiguration?"

"I...hey, who are you?"

McLuhan stops with the hand thing.

"Paul."

"No. I'm serious. Who are you...*really*?"

"I'm, em, Paul. Paul McCartney. The Beatle and all?"

"You're not."

"I am."

"You're not. Paul doesn't talk like that. He doesn't... He's not as..."

"There's more to Paul than meets the eye, man."

"Stop it. You're scaring me."

"Have you ever wondered why he never shows any signs of aging, for example?"

"Stop it."

"Oh, sure, a little gray hair like five years ago, and then...poof...nothing. Remember? And that baby face..."

"Stop it!"

"Exactly the same as a decade ago, isn't it...and as the decade before that. I mean, compare his holding-power to that of Keith Richards, you know, and what do you see?"

"I'm covering my ears here and whistling to myself."

"Freaky, isn't it?"

"Hmmmmm hmmmmmm..."

"I've got two words for you."

"I see your mouth moving but I refuse to listen."

"Tick tick."

"*Hmmmmmmmm hmmmmmmmm hmmmmmmmm...*"

"Tick tick. Tick tick."

"*Hmmmmmmmm hmmmmmmmm hmmmmmmmm...*"

268. NATURE IS NOT NICE

How many teenagers are left?

First four. Then three. Then two.

Now only one.

The most beautiful. Fair angel. Eighteen and mostly naked. Lace panties and bra. Bespattered with mud. Wet blond hair matted to face. Trickles of water and tears zigging down her cheeks. Trapped in the barn of the desolate farm. Stalked by Zodiac Killer, homicidal maniac.

Violent rainstorm crashing outside.

Lightning.

In each enormous flash a huge shadow looms closer.

She screams piercingly. She crawls. She stands. She sits, paralyzed by mortality.

Zodiac Killer wields a pitchfork in one hand and a whirring chainsaw in the other.

He towers over her.

He's laughing.

The teenager must learn how to lose gracefully.

Because in her back pocket she's carrying a nearly used-up tube of gash-red lipstick and, if she's not murdered right this minute, Zodiac Killer knows, she will drive to the coast two months hence to quietly reflect upon her past and contemplate her future options (a major in business at Slippery Rock Community College? a major in communications at Fairleigh Dickinson?) and that tube will accidentally work its way out of her back pocket and pop onto the sand where the cute little French boy who starred in that commercial for Zerp will, vacationing on Coney Island with his parents during his first holiday to the U.S. (in celebration of his ascending career), pick it up forty-one days later and chuck it as far as he can into the Atlantic Ocean on a reflexive whim.

Little will he comprehend as he does so, though, that that tube will comprise the last piece of human shit thrown into the ocean before all the human shit thrown into the ocean over all the millennia of human shit-in-the-ocean-throwing finally reaches some critical mass, generating a molecular flashpoint where all the nascent waste-nanites flushed down secret-lab toilets over the last decade off the coast of New Jersey will merge with various contraceptives, industrial sludge, artificial fruit juices for kids, and cheap metals (including that tube of gash-red lipstick) and become in one shocking burst sentient, nor that that mess's first thought will concern destroying the ignorant lower life forms hogging all the good dry space on the planet, meaning mostly humanoids, and hence launching a massive assault on the human race, which it will do by first sneaking up on and attacking unsuspecting swimmers, then unsuspecting surfers, then small-boaters, then large-shippers, and, on one momentous day in August, by loosing a blitzkrieg no one could foresee on Tokyo, New York, and London, resulting within fewer than four months in the earth having been turned into a big ball of very intelligent gray nano-goo.

3. PRIME: TIME: LIVE
Bad would have to be an understatement for how Ker feels.
Something evil has begun transpiring in his bowels. Plus his head feels like someone has inserted a hose through his left ear and pumped his cranial cavity full of pink insulation.
Plus, if he's not mistaken, he can't feel his feet anymore.
He thinks one word to himself: *bathroom*.
As he shakily rises to propel himself posthaste down the hall, the pounding at the front door commences.

172. AS SEEN ON TV
Tribal drums and primitive wails blossom.
Colors whirl.
Black men in grass skirts and jangling brass earrings, bracelets, and necklaces dance wildly around a bonfire, shaking spears, lifting knees, hooting and jabbering at the nightspirits.

Their earlobes hang to their jawbones.

Scars mark their cheeks.

Only the whites of their eyes show.

They leap and caper around this naked pale body tied to the ground, ready for the sacrifice, his arms stretched out to his sides, his legs wide apart, his anxious face alert... familiar...very familiar...

"Way-hate a sec here," Ker says aloud, halfway out of his bean-bag chair.

He leans forward, aware of sick sweat forming across his upper lip, squints, focuses, and sees...a-and sees...*himself* there, his own eyes looking back at him, terrified...

"Oh, *fuck*!!!!!"

13. HE DO THE POLICE IN DIFFERENT VOICES

Thomas Stearns Eliot, born in St. Louis on September 26, 1888, was one of the greatest

222. KNOW YOUR INNER CHILD

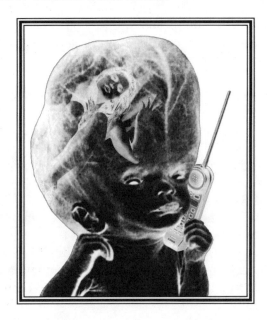

166. THE GREAT WHEEL SPINS

A car burns out of control. Upside down. A bus on top of it. An orange and black and umber and saffron fireball.

But whose car?

Where?

Under what circumstances?

Who's inside?

58. LOVEBOAT

It's too late.

The barrel-chested man in the black cowboy hat fires.

China crashes.

Crystal splinters.

A chair cracks against the floor.

Buh-but the mother in the white cowboy hat fires first.

With her tommy gun.

"*Uggghhhh!*" the barrel-chested man in the white cowboy hat cries, astounded, chest riddled with bullets. He slumps to his knees. "Mama..." he says, surprised.

Pitches forward.

Expires.

Mother laughs, embraces the barrel-chested man in the black cowboy hat, united with her lover at last.

99. NATURE IS NOT NICE

Ker starts off down the hall, something expanding in his bowels like a film of a blossoming black carnation, only the pounding at the front door gets louder and more insistent.

He groans, stops, turns, sort of shuffle-hops a couple of paces toward the living room, thinks better of it, turns, trots toward the bathroom, halts when the pounding erupts onto banging, begins worrying about Syndi again (it simply *has* to be time for her to get home...he needs to remember to glance at the clock in the bedroom as he passes), halts, cradles his belly like a pregnant woman, turns, shuffle-hops towards the front door, earnestly contemplates embarrassing himself in front of a stranger, concludes this couldn't be Syndi, she just wouldn't pound like that, turns, trots toward the bathroom, halts when he realizes she wouldn't pound like that *unless it was an emergency*, turns, shuffle-hops toward the front door, undoes the two bolts and chain and lock, cracks it open, and... *BLAM!!!*

In explodes Zodiac Killer, and, fuck, is he big...seven feet tall if an inch, and somehow that ski mask makes him look that much bigger, and the huge Bowie knife, too, which he's currently resting against Ker's throat, having with his forearm pinned Ker to the wall, and he's *smiling*...

"What have you done with Syndi?" Ker gurgles.

"That her name, huh? Cute thing..."

It strikes Ker he's never thought about Zodiac Killer's breath before, but now understands it has the same moisture and fecal reek as the air maybe two inches above a garbage dump on the outskirts of São Paulo on a hot summer's afternoon.

Ker gurgles some more in anger.

He shuts his eyes.

His bowels round the homestretch toward a pure plasma state.

Zodiac Killer chortles.

"She...*liked* it," he whispers tenderly in Ker's left ear, "is the thing. Asked for more. Died with a grin on her face. Know what she said before I hoisted her off the floor with the noose? Before she shat herself and died, grinning? 'Do me harder, sweetmeat. Do me...' Hic-hic-hic. Hic-hic-hic."

Ker opens his eyes.

A fairly large rivulet of blood is running out of Zodiac Killer's right nostril, is the first thing he sees.

Next he catches sight of that mean fire poker jutting from the homicidal maniac's head like some weird tv antenna.

Next he understands, very briefly, that, despite Zodiac Killer's breath, the guy really takes very good care of his teeth.

Because those teeth are all on display right now, as Zodiac Killer begins to squeak like a stepped-on mouse and spin around simultaneously, at which point Ker sort of slides down the wall like a slice of peanut-buttered bread, and he notices...hey, way-hate a sec here...Ker's suddenly wearing *lace panties and bra*...how the hell did *that* happen?...and his own pert teenage breasts fascinate him so much he can't help lifting a palm to cup one and cop a quick feel, only... *whump*...the chair shatters across Zodiac Killer's back...and there, above and left...who *is* that?...oh yeah, none other than the strikingly handsome nineteen-year-old baby-faced boy, Keane or Keir or Kendall or Kilian or Kipp or Kyle, whom Zodiac Killer shishkebabed earlier in the made-for-tv movie with another (and, in this case, barbed) redhot fire poker...and yet...and yet...he's *walking*...Keane or Keir or Kendall or Kilian or Kipp or Kyle's inching along, poker still sticking through his chest, not quite dead yet, still time for one last act of really impressive selfless heroism...

Flawless teeth in his grin, too, the drop-dead gorgeous guy raises two fingers to his forehead in a flip salute to posterity, gingerly releases an oily blue revolver from his back pocket, and takes aim.

"Yippie-kai-yay, motherfucker," he says.

And pulls the trigger.

But misses.

532. AS SEEN ON TV

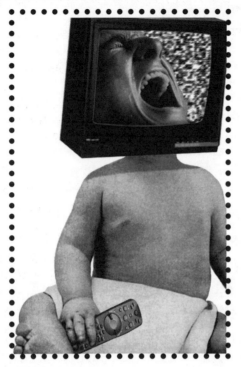

4. HE DO THE POLICE IN DIFFERENT VOICES

Rex Rory, flamboyant resident, releases an oily blue revolver from his back pocket, takes aim, and shoots Nona Nova, hospital nurse, once, just below her pert twentysomething left breast.

Not before Nona Nova, though, releases an oily blue revolver from her…where, exactly?…the logistics for this are somehow eluding Ker…and shoots him point blank in the groin.

Twice.

They fall to their respective knees.

"You rascally knave!" he shouts.

"You miserable miscreant!" she shouts.

"Strumpet!" he shouts, blood bubbling to his lips. .

"Beetle-headed whoreson!" she shouts, unable to catch her breath.

"Worsted-stocking beggar!" he shouts, falling over on his side.

"Reprobate cuckold!" she shouts, toppling over on her face.

"Mama?" the barrel-chested man in the black cowboy hat asks tentatively, poking his head into the women's restroom at the hospital. "Daddy? That you?"

249. THE DISCOVERY: CHANNEL

The monstrous great blue whale hangs under the ocean, ultramarine, pine green, indigo, gray, singing for its mate.

207. ADDRESS AT VISION 31

The great wheel spins. The audience shouts insanely. The game show host smiles confidently. Madge Moertel, fifty-seven, from Whitewater, Wisconsin, with a son in Attica, jumps up and down, her fat chugging, and claps her tiny hands in glee. The wheel spits fire. The wheel spits flame. Lights flash like lightning, and...slowly...

The wheel clicks to a halt, its arrow pointing to JACKPOT.

Sirens shriek. Buzzers trill. Alarms rattle.

Madge Moertel leaps into the air like an African chieftain. Bounds into the arms of the host. Her daughter rockets out of the audience and slaps onto the bi-hominidal cluster like a magnet.

Madge Moertel wins a dream vacation to Haiti.

Madge Moertel wins a year's supply of cat food for her dog.

Madge Moertel's face sprouts a flower. Her fingers sprout diamonds. Her eyes roll up under her lids.

She ignites.

A tremendous explosion follows: orange and black and umber and saffron fireball.

All around her people duck and cover.

33. WHITE QUEEN: BODILESSNESS: DARK

Which is when the ants come.

Ker lying flat on his back in his lace bra and panties beside his bean-bag chair in the living room, unable to move so much as an eyelid, watching the ceiling swarm with black ants. It seems like the ceiling doesn't even really exist anymore, that it's been insectivally devoured, that the ants have somehow *become* the ceiling through the act of ingesting it, a vibrant black undulating mass...which would have been awfully unpleasant in itself, no doubt, except that wasn't all.

The ants? They aren't just *above* his head. They're *inside* his head, too.

Ker can feel them skittering over the bones that comprise his skull where all that facial and cranial skin of his used to hang. He can feel them seething in place of the tongue in his mouth. They rush through his sinuses and over the backs of his eyeballs. They migrate up his otic canals, nibble through his ear drums, make burger of his hammers and anvils and stirrups and cochleae, single-file down his Eustachian tubes, and blast up his auditory nerves in a screech of B-film noise.

They assemble massive ant ranches in the creases of his cerebral cortex and the queen, obese and gloopy and gnarled like a big white turd, excavates his cerebellum and wraps her starched napkin around her horrible neck that joins her horrible cyborgish head to her horrible cyborgish thorax and picks up her mandibular knife and fork and goes to gustative town while birthing thousands of larval rice-eggs every minute, which is awful, godawful, but not as awfully godawful as when her troops force their way down Ker's esophagus in one big ramrod and then branch out into his lungs, ripping their way through mealy tissue and planting hundreds of larvae in some of the smaller less important semi-mucusy lung sacs, meaning Ker begins to cough, feeling like he can't catch his breath, till he forgets about that slight discomfort because they've also made their way into his heart, it feels like, though maybe it's just the lower reaches of his trachea, at which point he lurches into a full-blown grand-mal seizure, or what from his perspective feels like a full-blown grand-mal seizure, but can't be, in point of fact, since he still retains a semblance of consciousness.

Except what *really* scares him is when they get into his stomach, which about now feels like he's just gargled with a bottle of Sani-Flush laced with pins and thumbtacks, this flaming mass of damnation hissing into volcanic steam clouds when it hits meaty bottom and pretty much vaporizes his gall bladder and liver, and you don't even want to ask about his bile duct or poor little fried knot of duodenum, before whooming full-speed-ahead into his intestines, both large and small, like so much superheated plasma, causing him instantaneously to go liquid, simultaneously projectile vomiting blood-ants from his mouth, on the one hand, and spewing them in a hot muddy red jet from his anus, on the other, before what *really* spooks him happens, which is that he next just sort of goes—what's the word?—supernova.

One second he's there and the next he detonates, ka-*blam!*, covering the ceiling, which has become ants, and the walls, which have become ants, and the floors, which have become ants, with, weh-hell, ants and more ants and chunks of organs and flaps of skin and wads of hair, *his* organs and skin and hair, which now sprout compound eyes and six legs apiece and antennae and almost imperceptibly small stingers on their bottoms a-and start tooling away, single-file, a miniature battalion of buggish body parts marching in different directions, merging with the ant-soup all around them, the ant sea, the great ocean of Antlantis, a-and Ker lies there in his lace bra and panties, terrified, flat on his back, just watching his shredded selves disappear into the deep, into the dark, into that huge black nidus of bloodcurdling selflessness...

85. THE DISCOVERY: CHANNEL

"Ker?" Syndi asks tentatively, poking her head through the apartment door. "Ker? That you? Hey, happy birthday, lover!... Hey...but...uh, what's all *this*?"

128. SWEEPS: NEWS: TIME

We exchange memes in the night, with our bodies' erotic contact, just as bacteria exchange genes...

37. TIME FAMINE

200. THE LOVEBOAT

How many teenagers are left?
First four. Then three. Then two.
Now only one.
The most beautiful. Fair angel. Eighteen and mostly naked.

Lace panties and over-large Sick Poppies t-shirt of this black woodcut of this male bedbug stabbing its beak into this female bedbug's abdomen, preparing to release its sperm into her wound and bloodstream.

Wire-rimmed glasses bespattered with mud. Wet ponytail come undone. Honey hair matted to face.

It's…hey…it's *Syndi*!

Ker'd recognize her anywhere.

She's trapped in the barn of the desolate farm, stalked by Zodiac Killer, homicidal maniac.

Violent rainstorm crashing outside.

Lightning.

In each enormous flash a huge shadow looms closer.

She screams piercingly. She crawls. She stands. She sits, paralyzed by mortality, preparing to learn how to lose gracefully.

Zodiac Killer wields a pitchfork in one hand (Timex on wrist, you can't miss it) and a whirring chainsaw in the other.

He towers over her, laughing.

And then, unexpectedly, he chucks the pitchfork to his left, the chainsaw to his right.

Syndi cringes.

The chainsaw sputters and dies.

Zodiac Killer reaches up, grabs hold of his ski-mask, and tugs.

Beneath the mask is…is…weh-hell…it's *Ker*!

Syndi looks up, disbelieving at first, then a grin gradually spreads across her sweet countenance.

She breaks into laughter.

Stands, enters his parted arms.

"Ker," she says, "Ker…"

"It's okay, babe," Ker says, wearing his beige sweater with maroon stripes, "we made it."

They embrace.

They kiss.

On the lips.

Syndi reaches for his belt.

Ker reaches for her pert teenage breasts. For her firm belly. For the astonishing curve of her spine.

33. STEAL MY THOUGHTS FOR MONEY

97. LOVEBOAT: THE SEQUEL

Kerwin Penumbro feels like a million bucks.

000. IMMORTALITY: STEALTH

The phone rings.

Ker's eyes pop open.

He's been sleeping.

The room's dark except for the blue photonic haze from the Stealth's screen.

What time is it?

He reaches over and picks up the receiver.

"Myellow?"

"Mr. Penumbro?"

"Um, yeah?" he says, blinking himself awake.

"Mr. Penumbro, this is the police calling. You've been listed as next of kin on Syndi Shogunn's living will."

"What?"

"Ms. Shogunn was attacked in the parking lot of the

police station, Mr. Penumbro. The Zodiac Killer. She's in a coma at the hospital. You should get down here fast as you can..."

59. MIND AS CATHODE-RAY TUBE

164. DELTA: ART ALLUSION: SWEEPS

"Claude," Claude's father Clyde, man with the knowing smile, says to the cute little French boy from the soft-drink commercial as he steps off the wedge-shaped spaceship, all happy endings, "you know I love you."

"I love you too, dad," Claude says, wearing a beige sweater with maroon stripes.

They grin.
They embrace.
They kiss.
On the lips.
Claude reaches for Clyde's belt.
Clyde reaches for Claude's breasts. For his belly. For the astonishing curve of his spine.

13. UNCLE BUDDY'S PHANTOM FUNHOUSE

Man thus becomes the sex organs of the machine world just as the bee is of the plant world, permitting it to reproduce and constantly evolve to higher forms...

141. AS SEEN ON TV

The phone rings. Ker's eyes pop open. He's been sleeping. The room's dark except for the blue photonic haze from the Stealth's screen. What time is it? He reaches over and picks up the receiver. "Myellow?" "Ker?" "Um, yeah?" he says, blinking himself awake. "Ker, it's me." "Syndi?" "I'm running a little late. Be home in ten. Happy birthday, lover…"

177. SHE DO THE POLICE IN DIFFERENT VOICES

"I see a young woman," says psychic healer Abbey Rode, whose hair reminds Ker of a red rubber wig. Abbey has that slack-muscled serious-yet-utterly-accepting face that only drugged children and talk-show psychic healers have. Her eyes are closed in concentration. "Blond hair. Wire-rimmed glasses. She's on a farm, an isolated farm, a-and she will die tonight…"

209. PLAY: SIN

Zodiac Killer wields a pitchfork in one hand and a whirring chainsaw in the other.

He towers over her, laughing.

Syndi cringes.

The chainsaw flies down.

But misses.

Syndi leaps up, head-butting him in the groin, and he folds in pain. She yanks the pitchfork from his grip and drives it home, smack into the middle of his forehead.

Blood burbles from his lips.

He does that death-shudder thing people in low-budget made-for-tv movies do.

Syndi yanks out the pitchfork, reaches down, grabs hold of his ski-mask, and tugs.

Beneath the mask is…is…weh-hell…it's *Ker*!

Syndi stares, disbelieving at first, then a grin gradually spreads across her sweet countenance.

She breaks into laughter.

"About fucking time," she says.

999. HOPE FLOATS

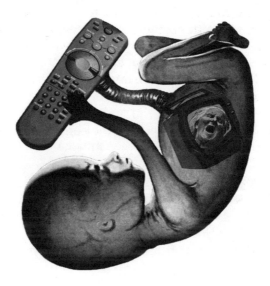

91. RUBBER WIG: ART: CRIMES

A woman with stelliform shoe-polish black hair's head derricks up and down in a man's naked lap.

The camera pans back.

A tv delivery man in khaki shirt is taking her from behind. Between his legs lies a second woman clearly wearing a cheap blond wig, lapping at the delivery man's genitals. Ker can't get a good look at her.

Buh-but, even in that wig, from this angle it looks just like...

217. ADDRESS AT VISION 31

The rock'n'roll star hangs under the ocean, ultra-marine, pine green, indigo, gray, singing for his mate. Bubbles sizzle out of his mouth. He raises two fingers to his forehead in a flip salute to posterity, unaware of the great white shark speeding in from behind him, flawless teeth in its grin.

14. SWEEPS: AS A SOAP OPERA: VANISHING POINT
　　Rex Rory, behind the wheel of one of the cars (though which is unclear), perspiration sparkling on his face, fury in his eyes, hatred at mouth corners, sticks his oily blue revolver out the window and squeezes off two shots.
　　The glowing green delta over the city wobbles.
　　Cut to the two children at the control panels, faces raided with terror, clutching each other and screaming.
　　The ship ignites.
　　A tremendous explosion follows: orange and black and umber and saffron fireball.
　　All across the city people duck and cover, thinking they are saved from the terrible invaders, but are wrong, because a single germ from planet Zerp will survive this nuclear blaze and drift down to earth where it will land on a fifty-dollar bill extended in the hand of one Mary Christmas to pay Dick Smoker for the crack cocaine she desperately needs to feed her recent addiction following her dad's recent bizarre demise (fetish encasement; lack of breathing tubes).
　　The germ will be passed via that bill across the country and then across the Atlantic to Berlin in the hands of a tourist named Gaye Powwers, where it will be exchanged for deutsche marks, during which process the germ will fall on the floor, where it will wait for six more months, till a little snot-nosed girl whose name isn't important will deliberately drop a wad of Bazooka bubble-gum on it, which a Pekingese named Fopson will later that day eat, passing the germ through his system unscathed while on a train bound for Prague, in which city he will deposit said germ by means of a well-formed pile of feces on his master's nice white rug at three a.m. for no particular reason, where his master's son, Fritz, distant ancestor of Franz Kafka's bastard child, at that stage where he has to taste everything,

will pick it up and actually take a bite first thing next morning, bringing the germ to consciousness as it hits those special stomach acids that spell H-U-M-A-N, at which point said germ will begin to multiply, releasing a plague that will cause people to see what happened to them four seconds ago, instead of what's happening to them right now, which will within the course of six years kill off the entire population of the planet by means of various ghastly accidents (car crashes, elevator mishaps, defenestration), paving the way for the next species to dominate the earth...not the cockroach, as it turns out, as many people believed, but the feathery-antennaed moth which, to this moment, had just been minding its own business, evolutionarily speaking.

777. BURNING MAN: THE SERIES

70. NATURE IS NOT NICE

Wile E. Coyote rises with great dignity, wipes the drop of whitish foam from his bottom with a handkerchief he gingerly produces...from where, exactly?...and hobbles toward the sunset as the Roadrunner, lounging by a boulder, smirk on his beak, rests his left heel on his right knee, lights a cigarette, and begins to dream of Paul McCartney in lace bra and panties.

1. THE DISCOVERY: CHANNEL

You wait one one-thousand, two one-thousand, three, trying to believe this can't be happening.

He plummets like a starfish.

There is no white bouquet of chute, no slowing of momentum, no sound save the whipping of wind far above the tiny red, white, and blue dot.

You watch him flap his arms and kick his legs.

You watch him speeding down, faster and faster... shooting down...humming down...hurtling straight for the jagged rocks and shallow river threading below.

The strong current.

The icy water.

The twisted bodies of those who tried and failed before him.

Seventy feet to go...forty...twenty...ten...six...a-and then: *whoosh*!

A-and then: *ahhhhh*!

A-and then and then and then: he pulls the backup cord and a beautiful orange and black and umber and saffron hang-glider unfolds from his parachute pouch like wings.

He skims the whitewater, zips over the jagged rocks, ascends above the pine trees in a miraculous arc, higher and higher, fair angel.

As he swoops up toward you, you see his face...his familiar face...his very familiar face. Beneath the lightning bolts on his helmet you make out Ker's features, those flawless teeth in his grin.

He zooms closer, raises two fingers to his forehead in a flip salute to posterity, and when you blink again he's...

Gone.

33. HOPE FLOATS